A large _____ _____ _____ _____ our house and honked its horn.

"That's me," I heard Akhil say. "He usually picks me up at my host family's house, but he said he could give me a lift from anywhere."

"So you gave him directions to my house," I said angrily. I didn't know who "he" was, but I was infuriated anyway.

"Well, yes, since this is where I am." Akhil blinked at me, looking both confused and innocent. I was now nearer to him than I had been in class, and I got a good look at the scratch-like scars on his neck and arms.

I pushed the curtains aside and took another look at the car. Its windows were tinted, so I couldn't see inside. "Who is 'he,' anyway?" I asked more nicely.

"It's the driver from the National Institutes of Health—I go every afternoon for the studies." Akhil stood up. "I'll see you tomorrow in school, then?"

Omar and I both said, "Yeah. Sure." We walked him to the door.

Omar called after him, "You must be studying some really cool stuff at NIH, huh?"

Akhil shook his head. "I'm not studying anything," he said simply. "They're studying me."

OTHER BOOKS YOU MAY ENJOY

the pack
elisa carbone

speak

An Imprint of Penguin Group (USA) Inc.

SPEAK

Published by the Penguin Group

Penguin Group (USA) Inc.,

345 Hudson Street, New York, New York 10014, U.S.A.

Penguin Group (Canada), 90 Eglinton Avenue East, Suite 700, Toronto, Ontario, Canada M4P 2Y3 (a division of Pearson Penguin Canada Inc.)

Penguin Books Ltd, 80 Strand, London WC2R 0RL, England

Penguin Ireland, 25 St Stephen's Green, Dublin 2, Ireland
(a division of Penguin Books Ltd)

Penguin Group (Australia), 250 Camberwell Road, Camberwell, Victoria 3124, Australia (a division of Pearson Australia Group Pty Ltd)

Penguin Books India Pvt Ltd, 11 Community Centre, Panchsheel Park, New Delhi - 110 017, India

Penguin Group (NZ), Cnr Airborne and Rosedale Roads, Albany, Auckland 1310, New Zealand (a division of Pearson New Zealand Ltd)

Penguin Books (South Africa) (Pty) Ltd, 24 Sturdee Avenue, Rosebank, Johannesburg 2196, South Africa

Registered Offices: Penguin Books Ltd, 80 Strand, London WC2R 0RL, England

First published in the United States of America by Viking,
a division of Penguin Putnam Books for Young Readers, 2003
Published by Speak, an imprint of Penguin Group (USA) Inc., 2006

1 3 5 7 9 10 8 6 4 2

THE LIBRARY OF CONGRESS HAS CATALOGED THE VIKING EDITION AS FOLLOWS:

Carbone, Elisa Lynn.

The pack / by Elisa Carbone.

p. cm.

Summary: Akhil Vyas, a new boy in school, reluctantly decides that in order to prevent a violent crime, he must tell Omar and Becky his secret.

ISBN 0-670-03619-6 (hc)

[1. Feral children—Fiction. 2. School violence—Fiction. 3. High schools—Fiction. 4. Wolves—Fiction. 5. Schools—Fiction.] I. Title.

PZ7.C1865 Pac 2003

[Fic]—dc21   2002009422

Speak ISBN 0-14-240535-3

Printed in the United States of America

Many thanks to my editor,
Tracy Gates,
for an adventuresome spirit,
along with expert guidance and support.

one

WHEN AKHIL VYAS showed up at school in early October, I thought he was, without a doubt, the weirdest person on earth. But on that cold December day, by the time the last police car left and the last ambulance pulled out of the school parking lot with tires screeching and siren wailing, I had begun to believe that he was the first truly sane person I'd ever known.

. . .

"Did you see his *neck*? And his *arms*? Good Lord, he looks like he's been in one too many razor blade fights!"

"And did you see his *eyes*? The way he stares? He gives me the creeps!"

That was Alana and Kathy talking. I knew I could stand nearby and listen because sometime back in middle school they designated me invisible. As goddesses of their own domain, which consists of themselves and anyone they decide is cool enough for them to associate with, they pass judgment on everyone else. They were now passing judgment on the new kid.

But I knew they only had part of the truth about him. They only ever have part of the truth about people. Like last year I saw them at lunch—Alana had borrowed some kid's glasses and in a fake Tennessee accent she was saying, "The reason I'm so damn *fat* is that I eat too much lard and drink too much Mountain Dew, that's all!" The truth is I only have a Tennessee accent when I first get back to school after visiting down home during summer break.

So I figured when I finally met up with this Akhil Vyas—whose name sounded to me like he was from Nepal or India or something—that he might be a little odd, but nothing to jump up and down about. I was wrong.

Second period English was when I first saw him. Jet-black hair. Shoulders hunched. Long, spindly arms and legs that made him look like a scarecrow—a cinnamon-colored scarecrow who'd been through a meat grinder some years ago and had healed up with raised scars like crisscross scratches on almost every piece of him. And Alana was right. The way he stared with those dark eyes gave me the creeps.

He ambled over to the side of the room, walked in a small circle three times, and sat down on the floor. I covered my mouth to hide a snicker. Finally, somebody weirder than me for Alana and Kathy to gossip about.

"Mr. Vyas, please take a seat in a chair like everyone else."

It was Mr. Preston. So far, one month into the school year, he hadn't had to yell at anyone. He'd told us since this was Honors English, he expected us to conduct ourselves like adults so we could focus on great literature instead of discipline.

"No thank you, sir."

We all stared at Akhil Vyas. Not only was he arguing with Mr. Preston, but he also had a gorgeous British accent.

"All right, Mr. Vyas," Mr. Preston said more forcefully. "This is no longer a request, it's an order. Take a seat."

Akhil stared at him, unflinching. "I am comfortable here," he said, speaking slowly, his words measured. "Sir."

Mr. Preston hung his head and rubbed his temples like this was giving him a migraine. "They don't pay me enough to do this baby-sitting." He seemed to be talking to himself. "I'll have him put in the regular class so he can harass me with the other jerks. One honors class was all I asked for—one class where I don't have to do crowd control. . . ."

We were all silent, waiting for Mr. Preston to gather himself. It was kind of upsetting to see a teacher start to fall apart like that.

Finally, he took a deep breath. "You were to have read the first seven chapters of *My Ántonia*, were you not?"

There was rustling and unzipping as we all pulled out our books.

Akhil didn't cause any commotion for the rest of the class time. He just sat hunched over his books with no expression on his face. I decided to make sure I sat far away from him every day, so if Mr. Preston put us into discussion groups I wouldn't end up in Akhil's group. Sometimes I can be a weirdo magnet. A kid with no friends sees me and thinks, "Fat, shy, girl—she *must* need a friend," so they latch on and don't let go. That just makes the teasing from Alana and Kathy and their entourage a lot worse. And believe me, I did *not* need it to get any worse. I made a mental note to keep my distance from Akhil.

By lunchtime I heard people talking about how Akhil refused to sit in a chair in any of his classes, and by the time school let out I'd heard that Mrs. Briggs, who is a bitch and a half, had stood over him and ordered him into a seat, that he'd climbed into one with his feet tucked under him the same way he sat on the floor, and when she'd demanded that he put his feet down, he'd gotten up and walked out of the room.

As I was leaving to catch my bus, my friend Omar grabbed my arm.

"I'm coming over later, okay?" he called over the din of the crowded hallway.

"Sure," I called back.

He said, "I'm bringing . . ." something, but I didn't hear what because I lost him in the crowd.

Omar and I have been best friends since fifth grade. It seems like in high school a lot of kids have a pack of friends they hang with, but with me and Omar it was still just the two of us. Almost every day he rides his bike home—he hates buses and crowds—and ends up at my house sometime later in the afternoon. I used to wonder why Omar and I get along so well, because in a lot of ways we're different. He's in Honors Math, and I hate math. I read all the time, and he's not much into books. Not to mention the fact that most people choose best friends from their same gender. But recently I realized that we have one really big thing in common: We both live in two worlds, and don't really belong in either of them.

Omar's dad, who was black, was in the armed services and died in Desert Storm—the war that supposedly nobody died in. Omar lives with his mother and grandmother, who are white. Omar feels like he's different from them, even though they're his family. His dad's family all live in North Carolina, and he goes to stay with them for a few weeks every summer. He doesn't feel like he belongs there, either. His skin is almost as light as mine, but he *looks* black. He feels different from the white kids and different from the black kids, so he doesn't hang out with anybody much, except me, even though I know there are plenty of kids—white, black, Asian, Latino, or whatever—who would like him a lot because he's fun and enthusiastic and a loyal friend.

I, on the other hand, got dropped by the stork into the wrong family and then moved with them into the wrong neighborhood. It's not that I don't love my family, because I do, very much. Maybe if we'd stayed in Tennessee, where my parents grew up, I'd be more like my cousins down there, with interest in practical things like raising horses and getting married. But when the last coal mine closed, my dad decided to move up here to the suburbs of Washington, D.C., where we could get ahead, maybe even buy a house. And we could have, too, if my little brother, Sam, hadn't gotten hit by a car and cost us my dad's salary for the rest of his life just to get him to walk again.

So I go to school with rich kids who can't understand why I don't have a computer in my bedroom. And my parents ended up with a daughter who is interested in impractical things like reading Ernest Hemingway and Edna St. Vincent Millay, and sometimes staying up late at night to write poems that I always throw away because nobody at school asked for them and nobody at home would understand them.

By the time I got the school bus driver to let me off near the grocery store, picked up stuff for dinner because my mom would be spending the afternoon at physical therapy with Sam, and caught the city bus home, Omar's bike was already lying on our front lawn. I suddenly remembered he'd said he was bringing something, and wondered what it was. When he brought his pet rattlesnake last month, my dad asked him not to do that anymore.

I stomped up the front steps, backpack full of books on my back and two bags of groceries in my arms. Omar would be in the living room watching TV, waiting for me. My parents never did absorb the city way of locking our doors. They say we don't have anything to steal except a ten-year-old television set, so why bother?

"Hi, Omar," I called in the direction of the living room, and headed straight to the kitchen to dump the groceries.

"Hi, Becky," Omar called.

"Hello," came another male voice.

I froze. I set the groceries down, let my backpack drop onto the floor, then slowly walked to the living room, ready to chew Omar out for letting someone besides himself in when no one was home.

Omar was sprawled in an armchair, swigging soda from a can. On the floor, in front of the couch, sat Akhil Vyas.

I had no words. The weirdest kid ever to land on planet Earth ends up in *my* school, and then, just as I'm figuring out how to steer clear of him, Omar brings him to my house.

"What—?" I started, but I couldn't finish without being incredibly rude.

"Akhil once fought a leopard with his bare hands," said Omar.

"I saw you staring at me in literature class," said Akhil.

At that moment I could have said just about anything, including, "There's a sale on lingerie at Kmart," and it would not have made the conversation any stranger. Instead, I said nothing, glowered at Omar, and went back to the kitchen to put away the groceries.

Omar didn't even notice that I was fuming. He just stayed in the living room, chatting with Akhil. The conversation was about wild animals—one of Omar's great passions—and hunting, which Omar intends to take up this fall with my dad and Sam.

I'd just begun to come up with some really good ways to get rid of Akhil fast—either tell him I'd just set flea bombs and they were about to go off or go running out of the house screaming "Fire!" and then run back in and lock the doors—when a large black car pulled up in front of our house and honked its horn.

"That's me," I heard Akhil say.

I returned to the living room.

"He usually picks me up at my host family's house, but he said he could give me a lift from anywhere."

"So you gave him directions to *my house*," I said

angrily. I didn't even know who "he" was, but I was infuriated anyway.

"Well, yes, since this is where I am." Akhil blinked at me, looking both confused and innocent, and I suddenly felt bad for being so mean. I was now nearer to him than I had been in class, and I got a good look at the scratch-like scars on his neck and arms. I guessed that wrestling with a leopard could give you some serious scars. Except for one line down his right cheek, his face was mostly smooth.

I pushed the curtains aside and took another look at the car. Its windows were tinted, so I couldn't see inside. "Who is 'he,' anyway?" I asked more nicely.

"It's the driver from the National Institutes of Health—I go every afternoon for the studies." Akhil stood up. "I'll see you tomorrow in school, then?"

Omar and I both said, "Yeah. Sure." We walked him to the door.

As Akhil started down the flagstones toward the car, Omar called after him, "You must be studying some really cool stuff at NIH, huh?"

Akhil shook his head. "I'm not studying anything," he said simply. "They're studying me."

He climbed into the back seat of the black car with the dark tinted windows and, when he shut the door, disappeared from sight.

two

WHEN SAM WAS born his body was perfect. I was five years old when Mom brought him home from the hospital and let me hold him.

"He's our baby, Mama?" I asked. "Nobody can take him away from us?"

Mom and Dad said no, nobody could take him away.

They were wrong. Kyle Metzger almost did.

Sam's body was still perfect two years ago when he was eight and got on his bike to ride to his friend's house a few blocks away. That was the same day Kyle Metzger decided to "borrow" his father's BMW and go for a joyride with no license and no idea how to drive a car.

Kyle took a turn too fast, ran over the curb onto the sidewalk, and brought Sam and his bike up against a stone wall with enough force to crunch Sam's spine, break several bones, and lacerate about half of his body.

The lacerations and broken bones healed. But it has taken four spinal surgeries and two years of physical therapy to get Sam out of a wheelchair. And I don't think he'll ever ride a bike again.

Health insurance isn't something Dad could afford on his salary as a laborer for a contractor. So Mr. Metzger told Dad he'd make sure his auto insurance paid for Sam's medical bills. That worked fine until we reached the limit—somewhere around a million dollars—and then the bills became Dad's to pay. People say Dad should have sued, but Dad says how could he, when Mr. Metzger was so nice to make sure his insurance paid for so long? Omar told me he heard Mr. Metzger once talking and laughing with a neighbor saying, "You don't ever have to worry about being sued by a hillbilly—they think it's unneighborly!"

Mr. Metzger, as his son's attorney, made sure Kyle came out of the whole thing with a clean record. No "driving without a license" no "reckless driving." Apparently, last summer Kyle turned sixteen and got his driver's license like nothing had ever happened. And he still stares me down when he passes me in the halls between classes, as if I'm the one who did something wrong, as if I'm annoying him by going to the same school he does. On the first day of school, when I was confused about where my next class was, incredibly frustrated, feeling (and looking, I'm sure) like I was about to cry, he had the god-awful nerve to come up behind me and whisper, "*Loser.*" I have fantasized about running him over with my mom's Chevy *way* too many times.

Omar and I were still at the window, speculating about why NIH wanted to study Akhil, when Mom and Sam got home. Sam came up the walk with his uneven gait, his metal canes tapping the flagstones.

"Yo, Sammy," I greeted him, picked him up, and swung him around, canes and all. Sam is skinny like Dad, so he's easy to do that with.

"Becky, be *careful*." Mom came huffing up the walk after him. Mom and I are built somewhat the same. It's not that either of us is puffy fat, just kind of wide.

"Mom, he's not made of glass," I said. It's our usual argument. I think Sam should be allowed to roughhouse like other normal kids, and she's always afraid he'll get hurt again.

"Slap me five, dude." Omar held out his hand for Sam.

"Mom, can Omar and me look at my rifle?" Sam asked.

Dad got Sam a .243-caliber rifle for his tenth birthday, and Omar and Sam's new thing is to sit and drool over the gun and talk about the hunting trip Dad's taking them on in late November. They're only allowed to take the rifle out when there's an adult home, even though it's not ever loaded in the house.

"All right, bring it to the living room," said Mom. She sounded tired.

I went with her to the kitchen to help start dinner, but she shooed me away and said go visit with the boys.

"I'm going to get a buck my first day out," Sam was bragging. "Get him in my sights, sneak up real slow and quiet—"

"That's Bambicide, you know," I interrupted him.

"Becky, you take all the fun out of it," Sam whined.

"Omar, if you think wild animals are so cool, how come you want to kill them?" I asked. It's not that I think hunting is so bad—I love the venison steaks and deer burgers we eat for months after hunting season. I was just having fun teasing them. "What would Rob Rattler think if he knew you were shooting one of his family members?"

"Snakes are not related to deer," said Omar.

"You know what I mean—the family of the animal kingdom. . . ."

But Omar was taking aim at Mom's favorite lamp. "Do you think your dad will take us to do target practice sometime soon?"

"Sure," said Sam. "I need to sight my gun in anyway."

I'd lost them.

After that I sat and watched them, wondering why my best friend seemed more interested in my little brother and Akhil, the nerd from hell, than he did in me. Finally, Mom called Sam to do his homework, and they packed up the rifle.

"Becky, let's sit with Akhil at lunch tomorrow," said Omar. "We can ask him why they're studying him at NIH."

"Actually, I've planned my entire life, and Akhil just doesn't figure in," I said.

Omar gave me an annoyed stare. "Why don't you like him?" he demanded.

I thought a minute. I wanted to give him a real answer. "I'm already pretty close to the bottom of the food chain at school. If I start hanging out with Akhil, I'll be algae. Those girls will be merciless," I said.

Omar hung his arm around my neck and jostled me. "They're already merciless, and you've survived," he said. "Besides, I told him we'd all eat together."

I groaned. "Fine."

I knew there was no arguing with him. Omar is one stubborn human. And I didn't have to ask him why he was so interested in Akhil. The guy says he fought a frigging leopard! But I wanted to hear the details of that story to see if it sounded believable. I mean, can you *do* that without getting killed? At any rate, to someone like Omar, who eats, sleeps, and breathes Animal Planet, the Discovery Channel, and *National Geographic*, Akhil had, I was sure, already been elevated to the status of wild animal guru.

Through the front window I watched Omar get on his bike and wave good-bye to me. If my dad had watched the whole interaction he would have asked, "Did you get a ticket with that, sweetheart?" meaning I'd been neatly railroaded into something I'd had no intention of doing. I rested my head against the windowpane and sighed. At least this would make Alana and Kathy happy.

three

THE NEXT DAY, English class began the same as it had the day before, except this time Mr. Preston didn't say anything to Akhil about him sitting on the floor. Then, partway into a lecture on the symbolism of the snake in the prairie-dog nest, from the seventh chapter of *My Ántonia*, there came, from the direction where Akhil was sitting, a loud, resounding fart.

Everyone looked at Akhil. A few people snickered. Even Mr. Preston stopped in midsentence and stared at Akhil for a moment. But Akhil focused on his lecture notes and acted like nothing had happened.

Strangely, that was a comfort to me. At least he was normal enough to *act* like it wasn't him, I thought. I was appalled at what happened next.

First, the people closest to Akhil started to fan their noses, and a couple made coughing and choking sounds. Then Akhil looked up.

"Oh, sorry, that was a bad one, wasn't it?" he said nonchalantly.

I folded my arms and put my head down on my desk. *I can't sit with this guy at lunch*, I thought. *I can't handle the humiliation.*

When I raised my head again, Akhil was on his way out of the room and Mr. Preston had that "they don't pay me enough to put up with this" look on his face. He marched to the door and called down the hall after Akhil.

"Mr. Vyas, I did not hear you ask permission to leave my class."

"I'm on my way to the loo," came Akhil's strong voice with the thick British accent, sounding impatient.

"Yes, but you did not ask permission," said Mr. Preston.

"I have to ask permission to go to the loo?" Akhil sounded quite irritated.

"Of course! This is a high school, not a playground!" Mr. Preston was now shouting down the hall.

"Mr. Preston," Akhil's voice boomed, "may I please go take a shit?"

I heard doors opening along the hall as other teachers stuck their heads out to see what was going on. Everyone in our class, except me, cracked up laughing, and Mr. Preston slid back into the room, shut the door tight, and collapsed against it with his eyes closed.

The class quieted down and watched Mr. Preston.

"Miss Tuttle." He addressed me in a soft voice without opening his eyes. I froze inside. "I don't want to see that boy in my classroom again. Please wait for him outside the boy's room, and when he comes out, take him directly to the office. Tell Dr. Mack I want him transferred out of Honors English—preferably to a remedial class so that he won't be my student at all. Could you do that for me, please?"

When I stood to leave, my face was bright red. I kept my eyes on my feet as I walked out. Inwardly I cursed the fact that since the first grade, something about my personality has made teachers trust me to go on adult-type errands for them. This was by far the worst errand I'd ever been sent on.

I leaned against the wall, waiting for Akhil. What in the world was I supposed to say? "Dr. Mack will be demoting you to remedial English today—I'll be your escort"?

Before I had much time to think, the boy's room door swung open and Akhil marched out and headed toward the front doors of the school.

"Akhil." I ran after him. "Where are you going?"

He stopped and turned. "Oh, hello, Becky." He ran one hand through his thick black hair. "I don't know where I'm going, really. I had considered a matinee. Would you like to come?"

My eyes bugged out. "You're going to the *movies*?"

"I thought a good comedy might calm me down," he said. He fidgeted with his fingers.

"But you can't leave the school grounds," I said, then immediately felt stupid. Why talk to Akhil about rules when he obviously lived as though they didn't apply to him?

He looked around furtively. "The armed guards must have fallen asleep—quickly, if we run now we can make it!"

I couldn't help smiling.

"But I guess you don't want to create trouble for yourself," he said. "They're not kicking you out."

I shook my head slightly. "They're not kicking you out of—" I began.

"Isn't that what they sent you to tell me?" he asked.

A chill ran up my spine. How could he have known? "Mr. Preston just wants you out of Honors English," I said.

He nodded. "And Mrs. Briggs wants me out of Earth Science, and so on. Give them two days—I'll be out."

He sat down on the floor and leaned up against the wall. His eyes looked sad, and I noticed that he had rather nice, long lashes. I sat down next to him. "Didn't they have rules you had to follow at school in . . . wherever you're from?"

"England, and India before that, and yes, they have very strict rules. I went to school in England once when I was eight. Took them a day and a half to kick me out. But when I was coming here I wanted to immerse myself in U.S. culture, you know?" He made a dunking motion with both hands. "Make some friends and all that. Everyone said that in American high schools they put up with just about anything. They said I'd hardly be noticed."

I stifled a laugh.

"I guess I've been noticed," he said.

I nodded. "But where did you go to school, then?"

"Didn't."

I raised my eyebrows.

"Home tutors. Lessons with the doctors who study me. Time on my own to read. A top-notch education all-around," he said.

"Why do they study you?" The question was out of my mouth before I could stop it. Here I'd thought Omar was inconsiderate to want to ask, and I'd just blurted it out without thinking.

"Can't say," he answered.

That stopped me short. I felt my cheeks burn with embarrassment. "I'm sorry I asked," I said. "That was rude."

"No it wasn't," he said. "Everyone asks—at least everyone who bothers to talk to me. But they've not wanted me to tell, ever. Not here, or in Britain, or before that in India." He shrugged his shoulders. "Something about it becoming a problem with the media or some such. They don't want anything to take my time away from the studies."

I didn't want to risk asking another dumb question, so I changed the subject. "Maybe you could just let Mr. Preston put you in a remedial English class like he wants to, and everything will settle down and you can stay in our school," I suggested.

Akhil laughed. "Mr. Preston wants me in remedial English? I've read more Hemingway, Fitzgerald, and Steinbeck than he'll ever find the time for, and—"

"You've read Hemingway? And Fitzgerald? Didn't you *love The Great Gatsby*?" I was nearly breathless, I was so excited to find someone else who loved the great old writers.

The click-click of female teacher shoes coming down the hallway made me jump to my feet. Akhil stayed put. "Akhil, stand up," I whispered urgently.

"Don't want to," he said.

Mrs. Ramirez descended on us like a bird of prey. "What is going on?" she demanded.

"We were just discussing Fitzgerald and Steinbeck," Akhil said calmly. "We're in Honors English."

Mrs. Ramirez narrowed her eyes at him. "You're the new student. I've heard about you." She turned to me. "Becky, you're a good girl. You stay out of trouble, you hear me?"

I nodded nervously.

She left us and click-clicked the rest of her way down the hall.

"Are you coming to the office with me?" I asked sheepishly. "I'm supposed to bring you to Dr. Mack, the principal."

Akhil reached his hand up for mine and groaned. "Lord, what fools these mortals be!"

I pulled on his hand, helping him to stand. "You like Shakespeare too?" I asked.

"Absolutely." He grinned at me. "Not going to school has given me loads of time to read. I've read all the best stuff at least twice."

I scrunched up my nose. "I don't think you're going to fit in at remedial English," I said.

He shrugged. "I don't fit in anywhere."

four

WHEN I BROUGHT Akhil to Dr. Mack and told him why Akhil was there, Dr. Mack looked grim. Dr. Mack is new as principal this year. He's a fairly young, tall, white man, with a friendly air about him, and it seemed as though it was an effort for him to look so serious. He told me thank you and led Akhil into his office.

Akhil wasn't around at lunchtime. It wasn't until the next day, when we both showed up early for English, that I heard what happened.

"Dr. Mack read me the riot act," said Akhil. "He said I had to follow all the rules, etcetera. But in the afternoon I talked to Dr. Lau—he's the head of the research division I work with at NIH. I told him that if they forced me to sit in a chair or put me into remedial English, or tried to remove me from school altogether, I would have to insist on returning to England. Of course, he doesn't want to lose me as a specimen, so he had a word with Dr. Mack, and . . ." He held his arms out, palms up, and lifted his chin. "I'm untouchable!"

I was stunned. "You *blackmailed* Dr. Lau so you could stay in school?"

"I wouldn't call it blackmail." Akhil tilted his head and frowned, seeming to search for a nicer word. "I'd call it coercion."

I gave him an exasperated stare.

"Come on, now," he said, "what fun would literature class be without me?"

I let a slight smile peek through. "But why do you want to go to school so badly?" I asked. "I thought about how you've gotten to spend your days reading. I would *love* to do that! I think I'd learn more too."

"There's no doubt you'd learn more," he said. "But here I get to learn about *people*."

I grimaced. "Yeah. About how obnoxious most of them are."

"Exactly," he said, grinning. "It's absolutely fascinating."

It suddenly struck me how unfair it would be if Akhil got to skip most of the rules the rest of us had to follow just because he had friends in high places. I folded my arms over my chest. "So, do you think you can do whatever you want and it doesn't matter? You can still get expelled, you know."

He gave me a pitiful look. "For *farting*?"

I punched him in the arm, and Mr. Preston called class to order.

• • •

The lunchroom was crowded and noisy, and Akhil hadn't showed up at our appointed meeting table yet.

"He won't follow teachers' rules, but he does whatever the NIH people tell him to do," Omar said, leaning in close to me. "I think it's suspicious."

"Suspicious of *what*?" I asked, annoyed.

"Maybe they've threatened him," said Omar.

I rolled my eyes. "Maybe he does what you ask him to if he respects you. He let me take him to Dr. Mack."

Omar lowered his voice. "Maybe the NIH people installed a computer chip under his skin and they control him with it. Maybe if he tries to tell anyone what they're studying him for, zap!"—he punched one fist at the air—"they cause him great pain."

"Omar, stop it!" I snapped. "He said it had something to do with the media—like they don't want reporters crawling around him all the time or something. Give it a rest, will you?"

Omar balked. "A couple of days ago you couldn't stand the guy, now you're his defender?"

I sat up straighter. "I got to know him a bit and now"—I chose my words carefully—"I think he's . . . interesting. I don't think we should pressure him about the NIH thing."

"Maybe he'll tell us if we promise not to leak it to the media," he suggested.

"Omar!"

We both pasted smiles on our faces as Akhil pulled out a chair and sat, cross-legged, next to Omar.

"Sorry, man, I can't tell you no matter what," said Akhil.

I blushed, and Omar slumped in his seat.

"Isn't anyone eating?" Akhil asked.

"We were waiting for you," I said.

We got in the food line. A minute later, Kyle Metzger and his friend Rudy got in line behind us. Kyle is tall, pale, and freckled. Rudy is a full head shorter and stocky, with close-cropped brown hair. I turned away from them and felt my jaw tighten.

"Look at that, Rudy, here's three of them right here," said Kyle.

Omar took one look at my face and turned to Kyle and Rudy. "You're in the wrong lunch," he said. "Unless you got put back a grade."

"Oh-oh. You going to tell on us?" Kyle asked in a mock-worried tone.

"No, but I am going to help you out the door if you don't leave on your own," said Omar calmly.

The line moved forward. Omar stayed put. Kyle would have had to go around him to stay with the line.

"Hey, Kyle," somebody called. "You flunk out of tenth grade already? What're you doing eating with the freshmen?"

Apparently, Kyle and Rudy decided it wasn't worth skipping class and taking two lunch periods if they were going to be harassed by ninth graders the entire time. Omar rejoined us in line.

I looked up at him. "Thanks," I said.

He tugged my hair gently. "No problem," he said. "I knew he'd ruin your digestion."

"Not one of your favorite people?" Akhil asked.

"We'll explain it to you later," said Omar.

We got our food and went back to our table.

"Hey Akhil," I said as we sat down. "How exactly did you fight that leopard?"

Akhil looked uncomfortable. "Oh, it was nothing, really, just a"—he tapped his knuckles against his head— "knock on the noggin with a rock and he was done for."

"Isn't that *amazing*, Becky? No gun or spear or any-thing—just a rock!" Omar was in awe all over again, hearing the story a second time.

"Was he attacking you or what?" I asked. I could see that Akhil had started to squirm, but I didn't think it was because the story was painful to retell, so I pressed him. "I mean, how did it happen?"

Akhil glanced nervously at Omar. "Oh, all right, I'll tell you. But you may decide to disown me."

"No way," said Omar.

Akhil took a deep breath. "It was on a group camp trip to a wild game park. I was nine. I smuggled in my slingshot and a rock the size of Ireland, and shot the poor bugger as we drove by him in the bus. He was unconscious for hours. I was expelled from the camp, needless to say." He looked from me to Omar sheepishly.

Omar laughed until he had tears in his eyes. He clapped Akhil on the back. "That's great, man. I like it even better than the way I'd imagined it, with you wrestling a leopard in the wild!"

"I admit, I was trying to impress you, since we'd just met and all," said Akhil.

I was perplexed. "But Akhil, I thought that was how you got all your scars—wrestling with Simba, you know?"

Akhil looked down at his arms, and I hoped I hadn't embarrassed him. "No." He hesitated. "Those are from . . . something else."

There was a moment of tense silence, then Omar piped up with more questions. "So, what did your parents think about you beaning the leopard? And where do they live, anyway? Do they ever get to come visit you at your host family's house?"

I watched him do it. He threw his hand up, knocked over his drink, then jumped to his feet and cried, "Napkins! I'll get them." And off he went.

I leveled my gaze at Omar. "Don't ask him anything else about his parents," I said in a low voice. "I don't want my drink to go flying too."

Omar widened his eyes like he'd gotten the hint. When Akhil returned we helped him mop up the spill.

To his credit, Omar then expertly changed the subject. "So, I was thinking. Hunting is kind of like you nailing that leopard from the bus—there's no bravery to it, really. Just sit there real quiet till a poor defenseless deer walks up, then *pow*, shoot him before he has a chance to run away." He got a faraway look in his eyes, the way he does when he's about to get philosophical. "Maybe I should go hunting during bow season instead of gun season. That way me and the deer would be more evenly matched."

"How about slingshot season?" I suggested. "Or you could go bear hunting during run-away-screaming season."

Omar gave Akhil a bland look. "She doesn't like hunting," he said.

"A vegetarian are you, then?" Akhil asked.

We all looked down at my mostly eaten hamburger. I gave a weak smile and was very thankful when the end-of-lunch bell rang.

five

THE BEST PART about weekends is that I get to read. Sometimes I lie in the hammock out back and read all day. If the book is good, it's like heaven. But I like hanging with Omar too. Except every month or so his mom gets him to help her with all the "manly" jobs around the house and yard, and so I don't see him.

Omar was being a manly man that second weekend in October, after Akhil had arrived. And I was restless—not in a reading mood at all. By Sunday noon I'd already finished my homework, helped my mom with some cleaning, played miniature golf in the backyard with Dad and Sam (Sam balances with one of his canes and has an awesome one-handed putting shot), and was bored. I went up to my room and found myself standing in front of my mirror, my thoughts going something like this: *So what does he do on weekends? Does he lie in a hammock and read all day? Does he do stuff with his host family? Go to NIH? Why the heck are you wondering about him? You never wish you knew what Omar was doing every minute. I wonder if my face would look thinner if I pinned my hair back.* (Holding hair in a ponytail.) *Yuck. My hair is so straight—no body. Boring.* (Dropping ponytail.) *I wonder if he thinks I'm boring. He talks to you, doesn't he? I wonder if he thinks I'm interesting, but not pretty.* (Taking glasses off.) *Would I look better in contacts?* (Squinting.) *I can't tell—I can't see myself.* (Putting glasses back on.) *Never mind—no way we can afford contacts. What do you care if he thinks you're pretty?!? That's ridiculous. He's just another guy, like Omar.* (Turning sideways to mirror, pressing sweatshirt against tummy.) *There's lots of people fatter than me at school.* (Turning the other way, sucking in stomach.) *Well, maybe not lots. But large people date, have boyfriends, get married. . . . Good grief, now you're thinking about marriage? Get a grip, girl.* (Tousling hair back to original lank position, tugging on sweatshirt for greatest sacklike effect.) *He's certainly not wondering what you're doing this weekend.* (Stomping out of room to go find something better to do.)

I had asked my mom if I could get new sneakers, since mine were looking so ratty. She said if I hadn't outgrown them it was silly to buy new ones, and she got me a bottle of cheap white shoe polish instead. I ended up sitting in the backyard, listening to Dad and Sam talk golf shots, slathering layers of shoe polish on my sneakers until they looked, in my estimation, almost as good as new.

After a boring weekend, school can actually be refreshing. Monday morning I found myself really looking forward to English—and *not* because of *My Ántonia*.

I guess that's why my guard was down—not that I could have prevented anything by having my guard up. I just should have known that Alana would never *honestly* say anything nice to me.

I was pulling things out of my locker before school, sort of humming to myself. Alana stopped near me and said, "Nice shoes." Sure, I noticed that she was trying hard not to laugh, but that was no reason for *me* to be rude. I said "thanks," and went on about my business. And yeah, I did notice Kathy coming down the hall walking kind of funny. But I didn't take that as a signal to run. Then all of a sudden, Kathy bumped into me and stepped hard on my right foot. They both ran off down the hall, laughing. They called back over their shoulders, "Nice shoes, Becky!"

When I looked down I saw what they'd done. My right sneaker had a thick brown smear of mud on it. Kathy must have carried it all the way in from outside on the bottom of her shoe just for me.

I washed it off as best I could but ended up with one wet brownish sneaker. It wasn't the most comfortable thing in the world.

That definitely took the wind out of my sails, so when I got to English class I was grumpy. I didn't even fully appreciate the fact that the first thing Akhil said to me was, "So, what did you do this weekend? I thought about calling you."

I answered like a typical teenager, "Oh, nothing." What was I supposed to say? "The highlight of my weekend was when I put four coats of white shoe polish on my sneakers, which now look like they've been stomped on by Godzilla"?

Class was shorter than usual because there was an assembly between first and second periods. As soon as the bell rang, Akhil said, "Let's hurry—I want to get good seats."

"For a police department 'Just Say No to Drugs' lecture?" I asked, incredulous.

"For people-watching!" He grabbed my hand and pulled me along toward the gymnasium. The place was already starting to fill up—it was an all-school assembly—and Akhil dragged me up the bleacher steps almost to the top.

"There," he said. "Bird's-eye view."

I was panting, out of breath. "But everyone is so small down there," I said. "We can hardly see them.

"Good point." He grasped my hand again and dragged me *down* the bleacher steps to a midpoint. "Better?" he asked.

I was mostly interested in no more steps, so I said, "Perfect."

He spread his arms. "We have here before us the entire student body—except, of course, those who have taken this opportunity to go smoke marijuana out on the athletic field."

We sat down and he immediately started scanning the crowd of students milling below. "The drama unfolds. . . . " he began. "Aha—look. Trouble brewing."

I looked where he pointed. A tall guy with his hair in corn rows was having a very animated discussion with a girl in way tight jeans. As I watched, even though I couldn't hear them, I began to realize it wasn't just a discussion. It was an argument.

"They're boyfriend and girlfriend," I said.

"Yes. And he did something to make her mad," said Akhil.

"Yeah—he's in big trouble, and he's trying to get out of it. But I think it's going to be a while!"

"I think you're right." Akhil was scanning again. "Look there."

I followed his gaze and saw Alana, her blond hair falling perfectly down her back. *Oh great*, I thought. *Akhil is going to start ogling Alana*. I moved away from him on the bench.

"Let's call her Queen Bitch," said Akhil. "I've watched her before; totally self-absorbed, no regard for others' feelings, not very bright, or if she is intelligent, not using her brains at this particular time in her life."

A slow smile spread across my face. "Excellent assessment," I said, and moved back closer to him.

"See who she's talking to? The chap with arms so muscle-bound they won't hang down straight? What is he—wrestler, football, something like that?"

"Something like that," I said. "She's in our grade, he's an upperclassman." The boy was one of those short-haired white guys on some team or another. I don't keep up with school sports, so I think of them as nondescript jocks.

"Just as I suspected," said Akhil. "See how she's gazing up, loads of eye contact, and he's looking around like he's distracted? It's a status thing. She's trying to raise her status by getting attention from Upper-Class Sports Team Guy. He's confused, though. He's thinking: 'She's a babe—it could raise my status to be seen with her. But she's a *freshman*—definitely a downer for status. Better look like I'm uninterested.'"

"So *this* is why you wanted to stay in school?" I teased.

He nodded. "Your turn."

I saw two Muslim girls come in, walking close together, their colorful long dresses billowing and their eyes round and dark under their white head coverings. They found seats over on the edge of the bleachers. "They feel like they're on the fringe," I said. "They've probably been teased for being different since they were little kids, so they stick together for support and try not to be noticed."

"Sounds right to me," said Akhil. "What about the chap down there. The way he walks and moves his hands, do you think he's a bit of a poof?"

"A *what?*"

"A poof. That he likes boys instead of girls."

"Oh, you mean *gay*. Sure, that's David Kazinsky. He's president of the Gay Students Association. But I think they only have a few members—there don't seem to be many people who want to 'come out' by joining an association."

Akhil was scanning again. "There's your not-so-favorite person," he said.

Kyle and Rudy had just come in.

"Spare me," I said. "Do we have to analyze him?"

"Just one point," said Akhil. "You think of him as so big and bad, but look—watch his head, his eyes."

Kyle was walking with his head slightly down, glancing from side to side. It gave him the look of a scared animal.

"And you still have to tell me why you hate the guy so much," said Akhil.

"Another time," I said. "Let's talk about Rudy instead." Even thinking about Kyle Metzger gave me a stomachache.

"Yes, Rudy the short friend. A follower. He looks up

to Kyle—literally and figuratively. He's a bit of the bar-
nacle variety—has to latch onto someone to feel really
good."

A policeman had picked up the microphone and was
trying to get everyone to find a seat and settle down. I
spotted Omar and stood to wave so he could come sit
with us. During the officer's lecture the three of us tried
to be polite and listen, but it was much more fun to
point people out and analyze them in whispers, so we
did a lot of that too.

six

I HAD NOTICED Kyle's T-shirt. Lots of people had. But I never would have said anything to him about it. People with fuses that short just can't deal with any kind of challenge. So I could hardly believe it when I heard, "*'Aryan Power'*—what *is* your problem?"

It was between classes. The halls were crowded. I turned to look. Kyle was facing off with an older, meaty kid with short red hair.

"I got no problem. *You* got a problem?" Kyle got up in his face.

"Yeah," the red-haired kid nodded, looking like he was just deciding to get serious about this. "Where'd you get that shirt, from some store for delusional weird—"

The guy didn't get to finish his insult. Kyle swung a fist into his face. The guy staggered for a split second, felt blood drip from his nose, then lit into Kyle with a vengeance.

"Fight!" someone yelled, and "Get him, P-Rex!" A group began to gather, encircling the two boys.

Kyle flailed and punched, but P-Rex was older, bigger, and faster. I wanted to shout *Yes!* every time P-Rex slugged him.

Two security guards came racing down the hall with Dr. Mack. They grabbed the two boys and pulled them apart.

"You're looking at suspension, both of you," Dr. Mack bellowed.

"He started it!" Kyle cried and struggled against the security guard who was holding him.

"You don't call throwing the first punch 'starting it'?" P-Rex shook his head. "Man, you *are* delusional."

I swear, if the guard holding Kyle hadn't been about twice his size, the fight would have started all over again.

"To my office," Dr. Mack ordered, and marched down the hall.

"You don't want to mess with me! You've got no authority over me!" Kyle cried, but the security guard dragged him off anyway.

A round of applause broke out among the kids who had been watching. Either I'm not the only one who hates Kyle Metzger, or "Aryan Power" isn't exactly the kind of slogan people want circulating in our school, or both.

• • •

At lunch Omar and Akhil had already heard about the fight, and I filled them in on the eyewitness details.

"People actually applauded," I said. I started to squirt a package of ketchup over my French fries.

"And I heard P-Rex's nose might be broken and there was blood and snot pouring out all over the place," said Omar.

I stopped squirting ketchup. "Omar, could we move on from the gory details now, please?"

"Sure." Omar bit into his sandwich.

"So, you'll get a few days free of this person you dislike so much," Akhil said.

I shook my head. "Talk about untouchable. I heard that the principal from last year finally gave up. Whatever Kyle did—bringing alcohol to school, hacking into the school's computer system and changing grades—if the principal tried to suspend him, Mr. Metzger stepped in, found some legal loophole, and threatened to sue everybody and bankrupt the school system."

"His dad's a hotshot lawyer," said Omar. "They live in my neighborhood, in the big houses near our town house development. My mom heard it's because Mr. Metzger has this great career in law planned for Kyle, starting with Harvard Law School, and he'll never get in if he gets suspended. So whatever Kyle does, his father makes sure he gets nothing negative on his record."

"Ah, the modern legal system," said Akhil. "It's not what you did, it's who you know."

"Maybe Dr. Mack will be different," I suggested.

Omar shrugged.

"So now will you tell me why you personally dislike this guy so much?" Akhil asked.

Omar gave me a questioning look. I nodded, pushed my French fries away, and sat staring at the table while Omar recounted how Kyle had taken my brother's perfect young body away from him and replaced it with daily struggle and pain. When he was done, Akhil was staring at me with a look so fierce it scared me.

"In the old days, the people meted out punishment— an eye for an eye, a life for a life." Akhil said it slowly, still staring at me trancelike. "Maybe Kyle needs to have a little accident. A little spinal cord damage . . ."

The blood drained from my cheeks. "Akhil!" I said it loudly, as if to break a spell. Then, more softly, "I don't want to actually hurt anyone."

Akhil seemed to startle out of the fierceness. He blinked. His face softened, and he relaxed in his seat. "Are you going to finish your fries?" he asked.

I shoved the fries over to him. Strange social manners I could handle. Secret meetings with doctors at NIH—his business. But blood thirst for revenge?

I sat back in my chair and watched him eat. Inwardly, I cautioned myself. *There is still a lot about this boy that you don't know. Be careful. Be very, very careful.*

seven

"I KNOW WHY they're studying Akhil at NIH." The phone had rung at 10:30 P.M. on Saturday night. It was Omar, and I knew we had about two minutes to talk before my dad would come in to tell me it was way too late to be on the phone.

As much as Akhil had freaked me out with his suggestion of revenge against Kyle, and as much as I thought it was Akhil's business what he did at NIH, I was still very curious. "Okay, why?" I said.

"He's got ESP," said Omar.

I remembered how Akhil had known the gist of my mission when I met him outside the boy's room door that day. "How do you know?" I asked.

"He did it twice," said Omar.

His voice was hushed, like he didn't want his mom or grandma to hear. "First when we ate lunch, and then again on the way home."

My dad had taken Sam, Omar, and Akhil out into the country to do target practice. They'd just gotten home.

"*What* did he do twice?" I asked impatiently.

"Have ESP!" Omar sounded annoyed right back.

"Omar"—I lowered my voice—"pretend we're on a pay phone long-distance and you're out of change and you have exactly one minute to tell me this incredibly important thing before the operator cuts us off, which is actually the situation, except that my dad will act as the operator. Now we're down to thirty seconds. Will you please get to the point?"

"Okay. All right. First when we took out our bag lunches, I hadn't even opened mine yet—I mean the bag was still *closed*, and Akhil says, 'Ah, tuna on rye— are you going to eat the whole thing?'"

"Omar, did you happen to mention what you'd brought for lunch while you guys were driving? You do that sometimes, you know," I said.

There was silence on the other end of the phone. Then, "I don't think I did."

My dad popped his head in my bedroom door. "Becky, it's after ten, you shouldn't be on the phone," he said.

"Okay, Dad. It's Omar—he's just telling me about the day. Did you all have a good time?"

Dad came over, smoothed my hair, and kissed me on the cheek. "We had loads of fun, and I'm wore out. Tell Omar good night."

"One more minute?" I held up one finger.

"*One* more," he said. He shut my door on his way out.

"Okay, Omar. What was the second thing?"

Omar talked fast. "On the way home everybody had to take a leak, and we were still on the back roads, so your dad just pulled the car over near some woods. It was pitch black—no moon or anything—and Akhil and I started to walk down this little hill to get away from the road. All of a sudden Akhil shoots out his arm and hits me across the chest. 'Stop!' he says. 'Why?' I say. 'Copperhead,' he says. I couldn't see *anything*. Your dad comes from the car with Sam and a flashlight, and sure enough, there's a big fat copperhead right in front of me, curled up and flicking his tongue.

"Did you take him home with you?" I asked.

"Becky, get serious! The guy knew the snake was there even though we couldn't see a thing."

"Maybe he heard it," I suggested.

"Copperheads don't rattle or warn," he said.

"Listen, my minute is up. I'll talk to you tomorrow, okay?"

"Right," said Omar.

I hung up the phone just as my dad came to check on me again. He stood in my doorway, his brown baseball cap almost touching the top of the door jamb.

"Did you get your schoolwork done today like you wanted to, honey?" he asked.

"Yep," I said. I'd used an English paper as my excuse

for not going on the soda can–shooting excursion.

"Coming down for a snack?" he asked.

Late-night snacks are one of the best things Dad and I do together. We've even created some of our own specialties, like tuna fish and banana sandwiches, ham with mustard and peanut butter, and, my personal favorite, blue cheese and peanuts on low-fat crackers. Tonight we made popcorn and sprinkled Parmesan cheese over it.

"So, what did you think of Akhil?" I asked. I think a part of me was hoping Dad might narrow his eyes and say, "He's a strange boy, that one. You'd best steer clear of him—and I won't be taking him on any more Saturday outings, that's for sure." But hoping for my dad to be judgmental about someone is like hoping for a golden retriever to bite the mailman.

"Nice kid," said Dad. "Very polite—he's some kind of foreigner, right?"

I nodded. I wanted to ask "Did he act weird or show any signs of having ESP?" and "Last week he seemed to go into a bloodthirsty, revengeful trance when he heard what Kyle Metzger did to Sam. I don't know if I should trust him—what do you think?" But my dad is the kind of person who takes life as it comes and doesn't analyze it too much. He enjoys the good things and takes the bad things the way a boxer takes punches, but he doesn't think about any of it before it plops in his lap on the day it happens. It's not that he's not smart—he *is*. He just lives in the moment, and doesn't pick apart people's actions and personalities. If I asked him either of my questions he'd just say, "Well, honey, you know it takes all kinds to make up this world," and then he'd ask me if I thought the popcorn needed more cheese.

"The older boys kept Sam bug-eyed all day with stories about leopards and bears and such. I wager he'll be crawling into bed with your mother and me sometime tonight after a bad dream." Dad laughed. "But he had more fun than Christmas."

I smiled. I was glad Sam had had a good time.

"Do you think the popcorn needs more cheese?" Dad asked.

I sprinkled on some more and we took the bowl into the living room, where the television was on and Mom was asleep in a chair. Dad watched the news and I thought about Akhil. Did the boy have some horrible, violent side of his personality—is that what I caught a glimpse of in the cafeteria the other day? Is that why he'd never been allowed to go to school with other kids? And what were his scars really from? Was he the victim of terrible child abuse? Is that why he'd reacted so strongly when Omar asked him about his parents? Is *that* why they were studying him at NIH? Was he dangerous? Could he be trusted? Should I make sure he stayed away from my little brother? My fears began to spiral out of control, and I found myself munching pop-corn furiously. *Calm down,* I told myself. *Don't jump to conclusions. He made one comment, one threat.*

I'm not much for keeping my mouth shut about things. I decided that Monday morning Akhil Vyas was going to get an earful.

eight

"I DIDN'T REALIZE she was *that* hard up for friends."

"I know. It's like they're the three misfit musketeers."

"The three stooges."

"The three *losers!*"

Alana and Kathy were at the sinks, I was in a stall, and I wasn't sure if they knew I was there. I shut my eyes tight. *This doesn't go on forever,* I assured myself. *Someday I'll be an English professor at a university and the other faculty members will not gossip about my weight, my choice of friends, or my family background. Until then I will keep my integrity. I will* not *barge out of this stall and call them bitches from hell, tell them they have the emotional maturity of cartoon characters, and threaten to punch their teeth out. I will not. I will not. I will not.*

I kept my eyes shut and waited for them to finish.

"That poor girl will *never* have a date," said Kathy. I could imagine her primping her auburn curls in the mirror as she said it. "Overeaters Anonymous, do I have a challenge for you!" They both went nearly hysterical laughing.

The bell rang, they left, and I raced out of the girls' room and down the hall to English. Mr. Preston stared at me a moment as I walked in late, something I never do, but he didn't say anything. He was already starting a discussion of *My Ántonia*. I glanced over at Akhil. I'd have to wait until lunch to talk to him. He sat cross-legged on the floor, like he always did, bent over his book and notebook, immersed in his thoughts. He rarely contributed to class discussions, but when he did, his comments were short and intelligent.

"So now we're up to the wedding—the story of Pavel and Peter, where we finally find out their deep, terrible secret," Mr. Preston was saying. "That was quite a horrifying scene, don't you think, where the wedding party and their horses are attacked and eaten by hungry wolves?"

There was a murmur of agreement in the class. One kid said, "That was *awesome*."

"Wolves don't attack humans." That was Akhil. He'd said it simply and firmly.

"Oh, yes they do!" said Mr. Preston with a condescending laugh. "I think this is an excellent depiction of the kind of dangers people used to face from large predators only a century ago."

"Healthy wolves don't hunt people and they don't eat people. They never have," said Akhil, still calm but beginning to raise his voice.

Mr. Preston gave that nasty little laugh again. "Mr. Vyas, I'll invite you to read some of the literature about the days when men were carving out lives for their families among the wild beasts. You obviously have quite a hole in that vast literary résumé you supposedly possess."

"If the books say that wolves kill humans for food then they're nothing but bad, misinformed fiction by shoddy writers," Akhil snapped.

"Excuse me?" Mr. Preston wagged his copy of *My Ántonia* at Akhil. "Willa Cather is one of the great American novelists."

"She's a moron," Akhil nearly shouted.

Mr. Preston's eyes almost popped out of his head at that one. Kids were starting to squirm in their seats and whisper. I heard a couple of people say softly, "Go, Akhil," and "Tell it like it is."

"If people had bothered to learn the truth, maybe wolves wouldn't have been tortured and slaughtered!" Akhil was on his feet now, wagging his own copy of *My Ántonia* for emphasis. He had that scary, intense look in his eyes—the same one he'd had when he'd suggested we punish Kyle Metzger. My stomach tightened. "This is a crime, do you understand me?" Akhil held the book up in the air and looked around the room. "How many wolves have been bludgeoned to death or dynamited with their pups in their own dens because irresponsible writers convince people that they're bloodthirsty monsters?"

Akhil cocked his arm back and hurled the novel. Mr. Preston jumped to the side, though it wouldn't have hit him, and it bounced off his desk. There was a moment when no one moved. Then Akhil marched past Mr. Preston and out the door.

Before I was totally aware of what I was doing, I was on my feet, following Akhil down the hall. He went to the nearest school exit and shoved open the doors. I followed him outside. There, we both stopped. The sunlight, breeze, and birdsongs calmed both of us. We stared at each other.

"I don't understand," I said after a time. "What is it that happens to you—you get so angry, it looks like you want to kill someone. You did it last week in the cafeteria, and again today . . ."

He gazed at me, his eyes clear. "Don't you ever feel that something is just so *wrong*, that you want to force it right? Like with what that Metzger kid did to your brother—that was *wrong*. Yes, part of me would like to mess him up, leave him in a wheelchair, see how he likes it. I won't *do* it. But when you first told me, I wanted to. Haven't you ever had thoughts like that?"

I felt the color rise to my cheeks. Of course I had. In

my imagination I'd smashed a car into Kyle Metzger a thousand times. And I had thoroughly enjoyed watching him get beat up. "Yes," I said softly.

Akhil looked across the courtyard at some trees swaying in the wind. "And about the wolves . . . you wouldn't understand. No one can understand."

"Try me," I said.

He looked like I'd surprised him. He frowned. "I guess it's the same as with your little brother," he said thoughtfully. "When you love someone—or something—you can't stand it when there's injustice done."

"So you're really into wolves?" I asked.

He smiled a little sadly. "I suppose you could say that."

I took a deep breath. "Omar thinks you have ESP," I blurted out.

Akhil leaned his back against the brick wall of the school, closed his eyes, and pressed his fingertips to his forehead. "Let's see . . . right now Mr. Preston is furious at me and he's trying to get a discussion going, but it's not working very well." He opened his eyes. "How's that?"

I crossed my arms over my chest. "Seriously," I said. "He thinks that's why they're studying you at NIH."

Akhil looked sad again. "I can't tell you why they're studying me." He said it in a tired way, as if he was tired of saying it and tired of the truth of it. He reached out and grasped my hand. I let my arms slip out of their folded, guarded position. He traced my fingers with one of his. "Sometimes I feel I want to tell you," he said.

A thrill went through me—either from the offer of his secret, or from his touch, or both. Embarrassed, I snatched my hand away.

"Well," I said, swinging my arms, "I hate to say it, but throwing a book at a teacher is much worse than farting. I think you're looking at a suspension here."

Akhil laughed. "Good. I could use the reading time."

We went back inside and I walked with him to Dr. Mack's office.

"Shall I tell Mr. Preston I turned you in?" I asked.

"No. Tell him I turned myself in. I shouldn't have expected him to know more than anyone else does about wolves. Tell him I'm sorry."

I was astounded.

"You see?" he said. "I am reasonable when I'm not enraged."

I narrowed my eyes at him. "Yes, but you're *very* scary when you are enraged."

"Sometimes that's a good thing," he said. He winked at me and opened the door to the office. "Oh, and if I'd actually thrown that book *at* Mr. Preston—"

"You would have hit him," I said.

"Exactly," said Akhil, and he disappeared into the office.

nine

AKHIL GOT THREE days of suspension and had to apologize to Mr. Preston, which he did. Kyle Metzger, who had, it turned out, broken P-Rex's nose and yelled obscenities at Dr. Mack in his office, had only gotten a week of detention. Like Akhil says, it's not what you did, it's who you know.

"That Metzger kid is wacko," said Omar one day at lunch. "He even finds ways to make home economics weird."

"What did he do now?" I asked, not sure I wanted to hear the answer.

"We're making pillows—I'm making Humpty-Dumpty with a yellow body and a face sewn on and four little blue legs—I'm stuffing all of them so they'll be nice and fat. It's really cool." Omar took a large bite of his sandwich and smiled proudly through his lettuce.

"And?" I raised my eyebrows.

"And . . . I'm about half done," said Omar.

I sighed.

"Oh, right." Omar remembered his original point. "And the teacher said we can make whatever we want, so Metzger is making his pillow—all black—in the shape of a gun. He says it's a Glock. Says he ought to get a real one and shoot Dr. Mack because he has no clue what is fair, had no business giving him detention when the other kid picked the fight, and has no right to say he can't wear his Aryan Power T-shirt—that it is his inalienable right to believe whatever he wants and wear whatever he wants."

"He told you all this?" I asked.

"He sits near me and talks while we're sewing. It's not that he told *me*—he just said it loud enough so the people near him could hear."

"What did people say?" I asked.

"Nothing. We all kind of acted like we hadn't heard. It was too weird. *He's* too weird."

I shuddered. "Well thank God it's only a pillow," I said.

"Yeah," Omar agreed.

"By the way, Akhil doesn't have ESP," I said. "That's not why they're studying him."

Omar raised his eyebrows.

"I asked him, and he just made fun of me for thinking it," I said.

"How do you know he's not lying?" Omar asked.

I groaned. "Why don't you just be friends with him and stop prying?"

"Because I'm curious. And what about his parents? I think we should ask him about them again—this time when there's nothing nearby he can knock over and spill."

I cringed inside, remembering my fear that Akhil had been the victim of terrible child abuse. I wasn't sure I wanted to know anything about his parents. And it was obvious he didn't want to talk about them.

"Omar, I think you should leave him alone. . . ." I said. But I could see the stubbornness in Omar's face.

"Let's call him and see if he can come over after school," said Omar. "Don't you want to know how his suspension is going?"

The three of us converged on my house at three o'clock, and, as I suspected would happen, Omar descended on Akhil with questions about his family.

"I . . . don't . . . really have a family anymore," Akhil said haltingly. "I mean, I have my host family here."

"Not your host family." Omar pressed him. "What about your parents? Do they live back in England?"

Akhil shook his head but said nothing.

I tried to come to Akhil's aid by changing the subject. "So, have you been reading a lot with your time off from school?" I asked.

But Akhil hung his head and didn't answer. He picked at a scar on the back of one of his hands.

"Akhil, you don't have to tell us—" I began.

"They were murdered," Akhil said softly.

I gasped.

"Oh, man," said Omar.

"It was a while ago—almost ten years? I don't like to think about it. . . . I . . . I watched."

My stomach twisted. "Oh my God, Akhil. That's awful! Did they catch the killers? Did they go to prison?"

Akhil looked at me as if he hadn't understood my questions. "It happened in India," was all he said.

"I'm really sorry, man," said Omar. "And I'm sorry I pushed you to talk about it."

Akhil waved away Omar's apology. "You couldn't have known." He turned to me. "And yes, I've been reading—Hemingway. Rereading *The Old Man and the Sea*. I needed a lesson in perseverance."

I smiled weakly.

Akhil suddenly stood and clapped his hands. "So, no sense crying over the past. Would you two like to go out for something to eat?"

I was surprised by his quick change, but I was beginning to get used to Akhil's abrupt moods.

"It's a *really* long walk to McDonald's from here," I said.

Akhil pushed the curtains aside. "My driver is here— he's got nothing to do but wait until I go to NIH, so he might as well drive us somewhere. What do you say?"

Omar said, "Sure. Let's go to the Starlight Diner. I'm always hungry, and Becky can always eat."

I would have glared at Omar, but I was still staring wide-eyed at the black car with the tinted windows parked in front of my house. "He just waits for you?" I asked.

"Yes," said Akhil. "He's studying, I think. He doesn't mind. He's getting paid."

We crowded out the door to the car, and Akhil tapped on one tinted window. It opened slowly.

Akhil explained our mission. I heard the door locks snap, and the boys each opened a door. Akhil sat cross-legged on the front seat and Omar and I climbed in back. Akhil introduced us to his driver, a young, very dark, very friendly man named Mr. Nuamah. All the way to the Starlight Diner, Mr. Nuamah talked our ears off in a lovely, lilting accent about how he'd come here from Ghana and was working between semesters at George Washington University to save money for tuition, and hadn't we been able to get Mr. Vyas to tell us his big secret yet, and he hadn't been able to either. We pulled up in front of the silver railroad car with the pink neon sign, that looks like it had rolled right out of the 1950s.

"This is a great place," said Omar. "The best burgers and fries anywhere—and it's all retro, even the music. It's just like the fifties except that I can get served up front along with the white folks."

We slid onto the red vinyl seats of a booth. A waitress with a blond ponytail and acne came to take our orders.

"Three burgers," said Omar.

"How would you like them done?" the waitress asked.

"Medium well," I said.

"Medium rare," said Omar.

Akhil cleared his throat. "I'd like mine raw, please, but make sure it's well thawed if you're using frozen."

The waitress smirked. "Okay, buddy, how do you want yours, really."

"Raw," said Akhil politely.

She squinted at him, turned, and left.

"You'd better watch out, you may just get what you asked for," said Omar with a grin.

A round, bald guy in a grease-splattered apron showed up—the cook, no doubt—and stood over us. "June says somebody at this table is hassling her."

"No one is hassling her. We were just giving her our orders," said Akhil.

"She says one guy is insisting on raw burger—thawed," the cook said, eyeing the pad June had written on.

"Right," said Akhil.

The cook pointed at him. "That's you?"

Akhil nodded.

"You want your burger raw," he said with a smirk.

"Yes, sir," Akhil said nicely.

The man shifted his weight from one foot to the other. He frowned at the pad in his hand. He looked up at Akhil. "You want fries with that?" he asked.

As soon as the cook left, the three of us collapsed with laughter. "You want fries with that?" we mimicked over and over, and got more hysterical each time. Finally, we calmed down, and Omar said, "Hey, man, what are you going to do with the raw burger?"

"Eat it," said Akhil.

We both stared at him. We still thought he was doing this all as a prank, purely for comic relief.

"Yuck!" I screwed up my face and grabbed my throat.

"You've never heard of steak tartare?" Akhil sounded very defensive.

I suddenly realized he was serious, and remembered my manners. Omar seemed to do the same. He started flipping through the table jukebox. "What should we listen to?" he asked.

We played "I Heard It through the Grapevine" and "Stand by Me," ate our burgers without looking too closely at Akhil's, and ordered a burger to go for Mr. Nuamah before we left—medium well.

ten

LIKE PIECES OF a puzzle—that was the way things started falling into our lives, making no sense at all until the whole picture had come together. First, one Friday morning before school, Kyle Metzger came up behind me when I was at my locker. I stiffened. He got so close I could smell his deodorant.

"If you weren't so *stupid*, you could save yourself a lot of hassle, you know that?" He said it in an even, chilling tone.

I didn't look at him. He did not deserve my attention. And while insults that involve my looks and my family background can definitely get to me, one thing I'm sure of is that I am *not* stupid.

"It's not you, you know," Kyle continued. "It's who you hang with. You should ditch that black boyfriend of yours while you've still got time."

I hurriedly grabbed my books and took off down the hall and out of earshot. Why couldn't he just leave me alone? Hadn't he done enough to mess with my life?

And who was he talking about, anyway—what black boyfriend? Sure, Omar and I hung out all the time, but wasn't it obvious we were just good friends? Or was he talking about Akhil? I supposed that someone as ignorant as Kyle could mistake an East Indian for black, but *boyfriend*? I blushed at the thought of Kyle knowing what I had only begun to let *myself* know—that my feelings for Akhil carried an electricity that went well beyond friendship. If Kyle had it all figured out, it felt like a total invasion of my privacy.

"I *hate* Kyle Metzger," I told Omar in the hall between classes.

"You've got good reason to," Omar assured me. He didn't ask me any questions, for which I was thankful. It just felt good to vent. What I didn't know was that by the end of that day, all three of us would hate Kyle Metzger.

The after-school rush was a madhouse as usual. Omar came running up beside me. He was carrying a beat-up army surplus backpack, holding it away from his body like it was a snapping turtle, and looking more freaked than I've ever seen him.

"Go home and stay there," Omar ordered. "Akhil is on his way. I'll meet you both there."

I opened my mouth to ask him what the heck was going on, but he was off in the direction of the bike stands.

That backpack looked strangely familiar, but I couldn't place it. My stomach tied itself in a knot and stayed that way during the entire school bus ride home.

Omar made it to my house in record time, his own backpack on his back and the ratty army one strapped to the handlebars. He walked through the front door looking shell-shocked.

"I don't know . . ." he began, then trailed off. He slumped into a chair and let the green army pack drop to the floor. "I don't know what to do," he said.

I knelt in front of him and put my hands on his shoulders. "Omar, what in the world is going on?"

The black car pulled up and Akhil hurried up the flagstones and into the house. He quietly sat down on the floor near us.

"I . . . she asked me to return it," Omar was saying. "I said I lived in his neighborhood. He left it—I shouldn't have opened it."

I held his arms. He was shaking. "Okay, first of all, who is 'she'?" I asked.

"My home economics teacher," he said.

"And the pack belongs to . . . ?" Akhil asked.

Omar held Akhil's eyes for a brief moment. "Kyle Metzger."

"Okay, so Kyle left the pack in your home ec class, you said you lived near him, and you offered to return it to him," I said.

Omar nodded.

"And the problem is you opened it?" I asked.

"He saw something he shouldn't have seen," said Akhil. He reached for the pack, but Omar blocked him.

"If you've seen it, then we should too," said Akhil.

Omar sat back and Akhil pulled on the dirty leather straps to open the pack. He started pulling things out.

"*Calculus I, Intro to Computer Engineering, Physics.*" He plopped textbooks onto the floor. "Whoa—the chap is smart, huh?" He continued pulling out the contents of the pack. "Half-rotten chicken sandwich, Snickers bar, printout off the Internet, let's see: *Ridding the World of Inferiors for the Twenty-First Century.*"

Omar grasped his wrist. "It's horrifying. I read part of it—God, I wish I hadn't."

Akhil skimmed the page. "Lovely," he said. "Nazi Germany reborn, huh?"

He tried to hand the papers to me, but I grimaced. "Just tell me what it says," I told him.

"It's from . . . a hate group," Omar said. It looked as if it was paining him to talk. "They think anyone 'inferior' should be killed, the same way the Nazis did—handicapped people, even people with learning disabilities, homosexuals, Jews and . . . blacks. And they especially hate people they call 'race mixers.' They say their children are 'half-breeds.'"

I wanted to wrap Omar in a hug and block it all out.

Suddenly Kyle's words in the hallway came back to me: "You should ditch that black boyfriend of yours while you've still got time."

"What if he's thinking of acting on this stuff," I blurted out. "What if he *really* believes it?"

"That's why it freaks me out so much," said Omar. "I mean reading this trash is one thing, but these people want *action*. There's even a link at the bottom of the page for bomb-making instructions."

"And Kyle said something weird to me today," I said. "Something about 'while you've still got time.' The boy is *scary*. I want to know what he's up to."

Omar nodded. "Yeah. We need to find out."

Akhil had that fierce look in his eyes, and I was suddenly grateful for the violent, angry side of him. "Like the hunt," he said slowly. "We'll watch, gather information, wait, knowing that there is danger in waiting, but also danger in attacking too soon."

I blinked at him. Part of me had no idea what he was talking about. But, strangely, part of me completely understood.

Akhil unzipped the small compartment on the front of the backpack. He pulled out a bottle of pills. "Antidepressants . . ." he murmured. Then he pulled out pencils, pens, a compass, and keys. He held the keys dangling in the air. "I'd say his bedroom would be an excellent place to start gathering information, wouldn't you? What a shame he's lost his house keys. Now we'll have to make him another set." He slipped the keys into his own pocket.

"But—break into his *house*?" I whispered.

"Absolutely not," said Akhil "When one has the keys, it is not necessary to break in."

I felt dizzy. "What if we get *caught*?"

"What if Kyle Metzger hurts someone and we could have done something to prevent it?" he shot back.

"Let's go to the police, then," I said. "Right now, with this backpack and a list of all the weird things Kyle has said and done . . ."

"Great," said Omar. "We'll turn in the backpack to the police, and when Kyle wants to know who did it, the home ec teacher will say, 'Well, I gave it to Omar Wilcox to return to you. It must have been him.' And Kyle will say, 'Oh, you mean the half-breed,' and he and Rudy will ambush me some night and smash my head open with baseball bats. You didn't read this stuff Becky. It's *horrible*!"

I was having trouble breathing. "What are we looking for in his room, anyway. What do you expect to find?"

Akhil was as calm and intense as I was scared and queasy. "Equipment. Supplies. Notes. Plans. A weapon. Or, maybe nothing. Maybe he got an article off the Internet to show Rudy, and we'll find nothing but computer games and old fast-food wrappers. We'll have a look, that's all."

"Well, count me out," I said. I held up my hands and shook my head. "I'm not the breaking-and-entering type."

"Fair enough," said Akhil. He turned to Omar. "We'll copy the keys this afternoon. Mr. Nuamah can take us anywhere we need to go. Then, when you return the backpack, get them to invite you in. Talk to Kyle or his parents, whoever is there. Find out as much as you can, the layout of the house, his parents' work schedule, times when the house might be empty, stuff like that."

Omar nodded. "Like a salesman—get my foot in the door and don't let them close it until I've gotten what I need."

Akhil smiled slightly. "Like a wolf watching a herd of elk to find the weak link in the herd—the entry point."

I let out a very shaky breath. I was deathly afraid of Akhil's plan, but I was more afraid of doing nothing and finding out too late that Kyle was truly dangerous. I gripped the sides of my chair and felt my fingers go numb. "I'll go with you," I said.

eleven

MR. NUAMAH WAITED outside the drugstore while we got the keys copied, then drove us to Omar and Kyle's neighborhood. Akhil had him stop at a corner a couple of blocks from Kyle's house.

"We're going to visit a friend," Akhil explained. "I don't want him wondering about the car, so—"

"I got it, I got it," Mr. Nuamah assured Akhil. "I just purchased my books for next semester. I'll be here reading, very happily."

We had decided we would *all* go gather information, so we walked together down the street to Kyle's house. The last of the fall leaves clung to nearly bare branches overhead. I was shaking inside—the same kind of shaking that took hold of me when my dad told me Sam had been hit by a car and was in the hospital. My feet seemed to float above the sidewalk. By the time we got to Kyle's front door my tongue felt glued to the roof of my dry mouth.

Akhil rang the doorbell. At first there was silence

from behind the heavy carved wooden door. Then, finally, footsteps echoing on tile floor, and the door opening a crack.

"Hi, uh, Mrs. Metzger?" Omar said hesitantly.

It was dark inside the house, but I could see that the woman at the door was petite and thin, almost birdlike, with perfectly coifed brown hair and watery, overly made-up eyes. She nodded in answer to Omar's question, and her head trembled slightly.

"Is Kyle here—I have his pack. He left it at school today, and our teacher asked me to return it."

Mrs. Metzger suddenly became more talkative. "Oh, that boy would forget his pants in the morning if I didn't keep after him. He was so excited about his weekend away, I nearly had to sit on him to make sure he took warm clothes. Here." She opened the door farther to grab the pack. "I'll tell him you brought it by when he comes home Sunday."

She was closing the door. Inside my head a voice screamed *no!* We'd gathered no information, hadn't even gotten one foot inside the house.

"Mrs. Metzger!" I nearly shouted it just in time to keep her from shutting the door.

She blinked. "Yes, dear?" Then she squinted, as if she was taking a closer look at me. My chest tightened. Might she figure out I was Sam's sister? I made myself focus on our purpose: *Get in the house.* "May I use your bathroom?" I blurted out. It was the only thing that came to mind.

She looked annoyed, but she opened the door for me to come in. To my relief, the boys pushed in behind me without asking permission.

"Second door on the right," she said, looking even more annoyed that Omar and Akhil were now standing in her foyer.

I fled down the hallway, closed myself in the bathroom, and sat on the edge of the sink trying to calm down. At least all I had to do now was stay here for a few minutes while the boys started up a conversation with her.

I heard their voices fade into another part of the house and realized I would be able to locate Kyle's bedroom if it was on this hallway. I flushed the toilet and ran some water to make it all sound authentic, then tiptoed down the hall, peeking into rooms. The one with the black ceiling and walls covered with sci-fi posters—mostly of evil-looking humanoids running long swords through the chests of other evil-looking creatures—had to be his. First door on the left.

Omar and Akhil had gotten Mrs. Metzger laughing in the kitchen. On the counter were the remnants of what looked like a drink-mixing spree, and I realized that could well explain the tremor in the way she held her head.

"Well, listen, you have a lovely weekend," Akhil was saying. "Don't get into too much trouble." He had charmed her with his accent and wit, no doubt.

Mrs. Metzger flashed him a coquettish smile. *Good grief, she's flirting with him,* I thought. Was she one of those lonely wealthy housewives whose husbands ignore them? "You have a good weekend too, honey," she said.

My nervousness was eating away at my stomach. I was relieved when Omar said, "Thanks a lot," and she herded us to the door.

Outside, we ran to the end of the block. Then, out of sight of the house, we stopped to catch our breath.

"We got the scoop on the weekend," said Akhil.

"I think I'm going to throw up," I said.

"Do you want to go back to Mrs. Metzger' house?" Akhil suggested. "I'm sure she'll let you use the bathroom."

I punched him in the arm. "I got the location of his bedroom. First door on the left. Now you guys are on your own."

"Awesome," said Omar. "Everybody except the drunk old lady away for the weekend, and she'll be passed out by nine P.M. I say we go tomorrow night."

"Not *we*," I corrected. "*You*. Or *you guys*, plural." I slumped against a telephone pole. "Akhil, do you think Mr. Nuamah could drive me home now?" I asked weakly.

Akhil put his arm around me, and we all walked to

the car. "Becky, we'll get you home," he said. "But please don't abandon the pack."

"What *pack*? What are you talking about?" I asked.

But I didn't really listen to his answer, because I was thinking, *He's holding me closer than he has before, isn't he? Would he do this if I were just a buddy?*

"Becky," Akhil said close to my ear. I felt his breath against my neck, and it sent little shivers all through me. "You won't desert the pack, will you?"

"No," I said.

But I had no idea what he was talking about, and no idea what I was committing to.

twelve

OMAR AND I still spend the night at each other's houses from time to time, like we started doing when we were little kids. It's not that my parents are so progressive that they let me spend the night with a boy. It's that they're so old-fashioned, they think we're still like ten-year-olds. They just can't imagine their daughter being interested in boys. And with Omar, they're right. He's so much like another brother to me that I wouldn't ever be attracted to him. As far as the way Omar feels about me, I've seen the kind of girls he stops to look at and make comments about, and they're always cute little skinny things. I'm way too hefty to ever tempt Omar to think of romance.

So, when we planned to have a sleepover at Omar's house on Saturday night in order to be close to Kyle's house and do what we had to do, my dad said that would be fine. I felt perfectly normal spending the night at Omar's. I could have slept in the same *bed* with Omar and it wouldn't have felt inappropriate. It was Akhil I wasn't sure I should be having a sleepover with.

"Daddy, you know Akhil will be at Omar's on Saturday too, okay?" I asked. I think I was hoping he would forbid me to go, and then I wouldn't have to face the burglarizing extravaganza *or* the embarrassment of having a sleepover with a boy I couldn't keep my mind off of.

"That's nice, honey," said my dad. "Sounds like you'll have a great time."

Then I think he sensed my uneasiness.

"Omar's mamma and grandma will be there, right?" he asked.

I blushed. "Of *course*, Daddy!"

This was not helping. I touched my cheeks and tried to cool them with my hands. It was no big deal, I told myself. As long as I thought of myself as "one of the guys," I could get through the sleepover without too much embarrassment. And as far as searching Kyle's house was concerned, I was simply going to wait for them back at Omar's house and be there for moral support when they returned.

Waiting for Saturday night seemed to take forever. On Saturday morning at 6:00 A.M., Sam decided he was bored and needed his big sister to wake up and entertain him. I made pancakes, and we ate, dripping syrup, while we played Monopoly. At eight o'clock, Mom got up, and I said I'd better go back to bed, since I was having a sleepover tonight. But my brain kept going around in circles, worrying that Omar would get caught prowling around Kyle's house, or that Akhil would figure out how attracted I was to him and tell me to chill out. At ten I gave up trying to sleep and took a shower.

I offered to go with Mom while she took Sam to physical therapy, and get the grocery shopping done for Thanksgiving while they were at the clinic. But Mom said the sun was too bright and the food would get heated up in the car before she could get it home. Dad went to work to put in some overtime, and that left me with nothing to do but lie in the hammock and read— normally my absolute favorite thing to do, but today I just kept reading the same page of *The Grapes of Wrath* over and over again. Fortunately, I fell asleep in the hammock, or I never would have survived the rest of the afternoon.

By the time Mom and Sam got home I was packed and ready to leave for Omar's. On the drive over, Sam reminded me that it was almost time for the hunting trip.

"Tell Omar don't forget," said Sam. "First chance Daddy gets once gun season starts, we're heading to West Virginia."

"Oh, I'm sure he won't forget," I said.

"Tell Akhil to come too," said Sam.

"I'll let Akhil know he can come if he wants to," I said.

Mom parked the car in front of Omar's town house. I hugged Mom and Sam good-bye and promised Mom I'd say hello to Omar's family for her. I grabbed my overnight bag and my sleeping bag and marched up the front walk.

Omar's door had Indian corn hanging on it. I knocked, his grandma answered, and I spent my first half hour there catching her and Mrs. Wilcox up on my family news.

"We don't see you enough," said Mrs. Wilcox. She was a pretty woman with short-cropped blond hair and gray eyes. "You should come over more often."

I said I would. Then Omar whined that I was *his* friend and they should stop talking to me, and the boys dragged me upstairs to Omar's bedroom and shut the door.

"We have a problem," said Omar. He sat down heavily on his bed. Akhil plopped himself onto the floor, and I sat backward on Omar's desk chair, leaning my arms against the chair back.

"*You* do?" I asked innocently.

"No. *We* do," Omar shot back.

"Hey, I'm here for support," I said. "Leave me out of the illegal activities."

Omar sighed. "Well, let me just tell you the problem, okay?"

I felt myself putting on internal brakes—brakes

against their crazy ideas, against being railroaded into yet another scenario I wanted nothing to do with.

"I was totally into getting in Kyle's house tonight," Omar said. "I mean, I was excited about it, felt I could get the job done, you know?"

I nodded imperceptibly.

"Then I thought about the situation: middle-aged white female, alone at night, husband out of town, probably has a loaded gun in a nightstand drawer like everybody else in this city. . . . Suddenly she hears a noise—a young black male is in her house! Becky, she'll shoot me on sight, no questions asked."

I caught my breath. "My God, Omar, you're right. You can't go." I looked at Akhil. "So it falls to you."

But Akhil held out his arms, sleeves rolled up. Even with the raised whitish scars, the overall color was still cinnamon brown, even darker than Omar's. "I'm not much better," said Akhil. "Especially in the dark and when the holder of the gun has been drinking."

I rubbed my forehead. "So . . . we're making a new plan? Try to gather information without breaking into his house?" I wanted to feel relieved, but the way they were both looking at me sent a pang of fear through my gut. I glared at them. "No," I said firmly. "No frigging way." I shook my head, slammed on the brakes hard, but felt the railroad car slide forward anyway.

They said nothing, just waited. I closed my eyes,

folded my arms against the back of the chair, buried my face.

"Remember, it's not breaking in when you have the keys," Akhil said gently.

I groaned and, without looking up, held out one hand for the keys.

thirteen

"I'M INSANE," I said. "This is absolutely insane. I've gone off the deep end."

We'd told Omar's mom we were going out for a walk, which was true, and Omar and Akhil now flanked me as we walked down the dark street toward Kyle's house.

"I'll have a heart attack before I can get any information. You know how it is with fat people, we can have heart attacks at a very young age."

Akhil linked his arm through mine to steady me, but having him touch me only made me more unsteady. "Omar and I will open the door for you—very quietly. And we'll stay right there," Akhil was saying. "As soon as you step back outside, it'll be all over. We'll be there—if you've taken anything, you just hand it to us, and your part is over."

"*Taken* anything?!?" I said it too loud, and Omar shushed me.

"You know, plans, models, whatever you find that might help us figure out what the boy is up to," said Omar quietly.

"Great," I said. "So when he comes back on Sunday he'll go to his room and yell, 'Hey, Mom, have you seen my model of what the school will look like after I detonate five tons of dynamite in Dr. Mack's office?'"

They laughed but also looked at me funny, like they couldn't figure out how I'd switched from freaking out to joking around so quickly. I wasn't sure either. I think I was beyond all reasonable emotions.

When we arrived at Kyle's house, the lights in the family room were on, and even from outside we could hear the television.

"Okay, it's after ten," Akhil said, looking at his watch. "She's probably passed out in front of the TV, so don't let the lights and noise worry you." Akhil claimed to be an expert on the way alcoholics spend their evenings because he'd lived with a foster family for a while in England in which both the parents were raging drunks. I stood back from the door and let the boys work with the keys. I tried to take peaceful, slow breaths but hyperventilated instead. I pictured the foyer, the hallway, the kitchen and family room off to the side. I could easily get to the hallway without disturbing anyone in those other rooms. As I pictured it, I began to feel removed, as if I were floating above my body. A strange calm edged its way in past my fear, and when the door swung open silently, I slipped off my shoes and simply walked inside.

A drama show blared from the family room. The

hallway was dark. I glided to the first door on the left and stepped in. The black ceiling gave it an oppressive feeling. Omar had given me a tiny, pen-size flashlight, which I used to look over the stacks of books, papers, CDs, and video games. Stealthily, I opened notebooks, read lines of notes about engineering and physics, listened to my own breath in the quiet room.

Normal, I thought. These are normal things for a high school sophomore to have in his room. I opened his closet door and shined the small light on hanging shirts, pants, shelves with sweaters, then onto the floor to light up sneakers, dress shoes . . . a cardboard box of something that glittered. I knelt and looked closer into the box. My first thought was jewels—the boy is a jewel thief. But when I reached inside to pick some up, pain shot through my index finger. I snatched my hand back and saw that my finger was bleeding. I sucked on it. Glass. A box full of shards of broken glass.

The pain had sharpened my senses. *Hurry,* I told myself. *If there's something in here to find, you'd better find it* now. Instinctively, I reached under the piles of folded sweaters. First shelf, nothing. On the second shelf my hand touched the coils of a spiral ring notebook. *Right where I keep my diary too,* I thought. Ashamed to be prying, I flipped the notebook open to the first page. If it turned out to be poetry or love letters, I certainly didn't want to steal it. But if it could give us insight into his plans . . .

"Hit list," I read, then names and notations next to them. "Dora Melissano, LD, Natalie Borowski, wheelchair . . ." A wave of dizziness swayed me. I closed the notebook and tucked it under my arm. "Stay calm," I whispered. *Don't think about it. Focus on the moment— you'll be out of here in two minutes. Keep looking.*

I shined the weak flashlight over Kyle's bookshelves, past the ghoulish sci-fi posters, over his computer covered with gothic-looking stickers. Suddenly I heard footsteps—someone coming down the hall! My calmness exploded into terror. I hid the notebook under my shirt, dropped to the floor, laid myself flat against the carpet.

The footsteps padded to the bathroom. The bathroom light went on, then the door shut. I lay panting on the floor. Sweat dripped sideways across my face. The notebook dug into my ribs.

When the bathroom door opened and the light went out, I waited to the count of ten, then bolted.

I'd bolted too soon.

I screamed. He screamed. Then we both stood there staring at each other. I was frozen. I couldn't move or speak.

"What the hell is going on here?!" Mr. Metzger demanded.

I opened my mouth, as if I should answer.

His eyes flashed. "Claire," he shouted. "Get the phone. Call 911. There's a break-in."

I ran.

Down the hall, through the still open door, out into the night . . . "Run!" I cried in a hoarse whisper. I kept going. I heard the boys' footsteps behind me. I turned the corner, stepped on something sharp, yelped in pain, limped but kept running until I reached Omar's street. Then I turned and lashed out.

"You said he was out of town!" I cried. Omar was the closest, and I pounded my fists against his chest. Akhil grabbed my arms to stop me. I broke free and punched him as well. "Nobody home but the drunk old lady, you said!"

"Becky, be *quiet*!" Omar begged.

Now I was sobbing. "You said she'd be passed out, that there'd be no one else home," I wailed. I stopped hitting, hung my head, pulled at my hair.

We heard sirens in the distance. "They're coming to get us," I said. I was shaking all over.

Omar got brave and wrapped his arms around me. "Was there someone else home?" he asked quietly.

I nodded against his chest. "Kyle's father. God, even in an undershirt and pajama bottoms he looks like a mega-lawyer. He called the police."

"Oh, great," said Omar in despair.

I could tell they were looking at each other over my head. I hoped desperately that Akhil would have a comforting answer.

"Did you take anything?" Akhil asked.

With a sickening feeling I pulled the notebook from under my shirt. I'd clutched it there the whole time I ran. "It's either more horrible fantasies, or a very evil plan," I said as I handed it to him.

"You took nothing else?" he asked. "Nothing of value?"

"Of course I didn't take anything valuable!" I snapped.

"Does Mr. Metzger know who you are? Would he recognize you?" Akhil asked.

I thought a moment. I'd never actually met the man in person. Mostly my father dealt with him over the phone. And he didn't strike me as the kind of person who would care who I was. Whenever I happened to answer the phone when he called, he never said, "Becky, how are you? I'm so sorry this happened," or anything like that. It was always, "Mr. Tuttle, please. Tell him Mr. Metzger is calling." Why would he bother to find out what the sister of the boy his son ran over looked like?

I shook my head. "No. I don't think he knows me."

"Good," said Akhil. "Then we're probably okay. Do you want your shoes?"

He held out my sneakers. After all the stress of the evening, the gesture struck me as incredibly funny. It took both of them to calm me down so that I was not still laughing hysterically when we walked into Omar's house.

fourteen

I WAS STILL suppressing giggles when we found Omar's mother in the kitchen waiting up for us. And I'm sure my hair was a mess and my eyes were red from crying. Unfortunately, to Mrs. Wilcox, I appeared to be drunk.

"*What* have you three been up to?" she demanded, eyeing each of us.

"Just out walking, Mom," Omar replied. Boy, did he sound guilty.

"Come over here and let me smell your breath!" Mrs. Wilcox ordered.

That set me off on another round of giggles.

"Mom!" Omar whined. "You know I don't drink." But he obediently let his mother smell his breath.

"Good," she said. Then she gave me a questioning stare. "Becky, what have *you* been up to?"

Just out breaking into people's houses, I thought, and cracked up again. Akhil elbowed me hard. I strained to keep a straight face. "You can smell my breath too, Mrs. Wilcox," I said. "We honestly haven't been drinking. We wouldn't do that." There, I'd finally lasted ten seconds without laughing. "It's just . . ." *Please let me think of something intelligent.* "It's my allergies. Leaf mold. Omar tackled me in a pile of leaves. He still thinks I'm ten years old." I rubbed my eyes as if they itched and ran my fingers through my hair like I was still finding leaf fragments in it. I hated to lie to Omar's mother, but I didn't want her worrying about us.

"Omar!" his mother scolded. "Becky is a young lady now. You need to treat her with a little more respect."

"Thanks for telling him, Mrs. Wilcox," I said. "Somebody had to."

Omar looked like he was about to explode, not being able to defend himself. Upstairs he mimicked his mother. "Becky is a young lady now." He glowered at me. "Why'd you have to get me in trouble?"

I plunked myself down on his bed, my arms folded. "You deserved it," I said.

"Listen, I'm sorry," he said. "Mrs. Metzger was complaining about how much her husband travels, and how he'd left for yet another trip to Atlanta that morning. How were we supposed to know he'd be back by Saturday?"

I harrumphed, lifted my chin, and turned away.

Akhil murmured, "This is not good."

We both turned to him. He was sitting on the floor, flipping through the black notebook. "I mean, it's *very* good in that you got exactly what we needed. But it's not good. Not good at all." He turned the pages slowly, shaking his head.

Omar and I crowded behind him to see. The list ran down the page—names on the left, some we recognized as our classmates and teachers, some we didn't know— with short notations on the right, like "fag." There were the names of all the kids in remedial English, with "LD" next to their names for learning disabled. There was Katrina Bobcheck, the blind girl who'd won a national writing competition for our school, David Kazinsky, who had "come out" as gay and proud last year, Mrs. Goldman, a history teacher, with a "J" next to her name, Mr. Downie, Omar's math teacher, who had moved here from Jamaica, with the notation "N" in the right-hand column.

"It's just like the Nazis during World War Two," said Omar quietly. "In the camps, along with the Jews, they executed millions and millions of people they considered inferiors, like Polish Catholics, gypsies, homosexuals, blacks, the mentally and physically disabled . . . and that group Kyle is mixed up with think some of those people should be executed too."

"*Executed?*" My voice cracked.

"It says 'hit list,'" said Akhil.

"Oh, God," I breathed. I was afraid to look at the list, but I couldn't not look either. Akhil turned to the next page.

"Dr. Mack has a whole slew of offenses here," said Akhil.

Omar and I looked over his shoulder to read, "Dr. Mack . . . persecution for beliefs, unfair punishment, aiding the enemy." Akhil shook his head. "Some of the names are people he just hates for one reason or another, like Pete Rexman, P-Rex is on here, and Mrs. Briggs because she gave him a grade he didn't like in science last year. It seems to be a mixture of ideas he has absorbed from that hate group propaganda and his own anger at whoever has crossed him." He began to turn another page, but before we could see it, he slammed the book shut. A piece of paper came fluttering out onto the floor. I picked it up. "Enough!" it said in block letters. "Let's take America back now!"

"Why did you shut it?" Omar asked. His voice was monotone and challenging.

"I think we've seen enough, don't you?" Akhil said briskly.

"No," said Omar. He was staring at Akhil. "I didn't see quite enough."

"Anger is not going to help us now," said Akhil. "We need a plan."

"I want to know exactly what I'm planning against," said Omar. "Give me the book."

Akhil handed it to him reluctantly. Omar flipped through the pages and read out loud, "Omar Wilcox.

Half-breed." Then he narrowed his eyes at the page, and I thought they'd burn a hole in it. "Mrs. Wilcox." He clenched his jaw. "Race mixer. *Damn* him!" He shoved the notebook at me. "Here, Becky you're in there."

I looked down the list until my own name stared up at me. "Becky Tuttle." I blinked at the notation next to it. "Race mixer." But the words below hit me like a punch in the stomach. "Sam Tuttle" it said. "Gimp."

"Why?" I cried. "What is he doing? Why is he so horrible?"

"It's not just him," said Omar. "You saw the flyer— it's a whole organization. It's like all the Nazis who died in the forties have been reincarnated and want to start things up again."

I turned to Akhil "And you weren't on the list?"

"Of course I was," said Akhil. "I got an 'N.' All he knows is that he doesn't like me and I'm not white."

"What's he going to do with this?" I wailed.

"Nothing," said Akhil. A chill went through me as I recognized the familiar quiet rage in his voice. "Because we will stop him."

"Right," I said. "*Now* let's go to the police. Let's tell them everything we know, show them this notebook. They'll do something—take him out of school, send him to a juvenile detention center, *something*."

"Becky, are you crazy?" said Omar. "Since when is Kyle's father going to let that happen? And Kyle hasn't *done* anything. We, on the other hand, have committed burglary in order to get the notebook in the first place! Mr. Metzger is probably describing you to the police right now. The way Kyle's father works, *you* would end up in a juvenile detention center for breaking and entering, and we'd have done absolutely nothing to stop Kyle from doing whatever it is he wants to do."

I crumpled inside, despairing. Omar was right. I dropped onto the bed, hugged one of the pillows, rocked back and forth. We were silent as minutes ticked by. Finally I whispered, "Akhil?"

He turned to look at me, his eyes still filled with that intense, terrifying anger. Strangely, his rage was the only bit of comfort I could find at the moment. "How will we stop him?" I asked.

His voice was cold and hard. "We will rip out his throat."

fifteen

"WE CAN'T JUST kill him!" Omar objected.

"Akhil," I said firmly. "It's not an option, remember? You *feel* like you want to kill him, but we can't."

Akhil closed his eyes for a long moment. He seemed to be willing himself back to his normal state. Finally he took a deep breath. "I know," he said. He ran one hand through his hair in a gesture of frustration.

"We don't know for sure he plans to do anything," said Omar. "We need more information. Like, is there anyone else from school involved?

"What about this Rudy kid?" asked Akhil.

I remembered Kyle saying to Rudy, "Look, there's three of them right here." "Definitely Rudy," I said.

"Did you find anything else in his room—like a weapon, or anything suspicious?" Akhil asked.

I looked down at the flap of skin and dried blood on my index finger. "Glass," I said. "It was weird. In his closet he had a box of broken glass."

Omar and Akhil looked at each other, then shrugged.

"Other than that it was just the usual—clothes, video games, books, stuff like that," I said.

"Well, I think we should assume he's capable of doing something malicious," said Akhil. "He seems to feel little or no remorse about what he did to your brother."

Omar and I agreed.

"But still, venting your anger and bigotry into a notebook and actually hurting someone are two totally different things," Akhil continued. "I'd hate to mortally wound someone just because he's an asshole."

We all agreed.

"So we'll watch and wait," said Omar. "Keep gathering information."

"What's this?" I asked. I'd bravely picked up the notebook again and was reading. I'd come to a page that said only—"Code Word: Duo Duodecidem."

"Latin," said Akhil. "Two twelve."

"Maybe it's a date." said Omar. "February twelfth."

"If it is," I said, "and if this is more than venting—if it's actually a plan—then we've got a little over two months to do something about it."

• • •

Each day I waited, expecting the police to show up at my door and charge me with burglary. Only toward the end of the week did I begin to relax, to believe that when Mr. Metzger found that nothing of value was missing, he didn't have much of a case for police to investigate.

Omar did some information gathering on the Internet and found a whole network of hate groups a lot like the one Kyle's printout was from. He said he didn't really read the sites because they made him sick, but he did find an interesting article condemning the groups.

"They talk about the kind of person who gets into this stuff," said Omar. "Young people, mostly boys, angry at the world, no good role model at home. Sound like anyone we know?"

"Oh, yeah," I said.

"They latch onto one of these group leaders, and it makes them feel like they belong. It's somewhere to put their anger and something to believe in," Omar continued.

"Sounds like Nazi Germany all the way," said Akhil.

So now we knew a little better why Kyle had hooked up with this group, but we were no closer to knowing just how far he would go to live out his beliefs. And it didn't make us feel any safer.

My parents didn't know what had suddenly made it nearly impossible for me to sleep, eat, or concentrate on my schoolwork, but they did have an idea about what would make me feel better: a weekend hunting trip in West Virginia. I laughed out loud at the irony of it when my dad suggested it, because under normal circumstances I would have much rather stayed home. But with all of the fear that surrounded me each day at school, and followed me home each evening, I wanted nothing more than to get away. I wanted to get as far as possible from Kyle and Rudy and their cruel thoughts, and the possibility that those thoughts would lead to actions. I would have become a full-time hunter in the mountains of West Virginia if it meant I wouldn't have to face the threat from those boys anymore. So I gladly gathered up the Day-Glo orange vest and hat my dad had bought for me and packed my warmest outdoor clothes.

Akhil and Omar were both coming along. The two of them had spent the week tracking Kyle and Rudy, making a graph of what classes they had and where they were in the building at each hour of the day. But we promised not to talk about the hit list or anything having to do with Kyle or Rudy over the weekend. We all needed a break.

It would be fun to be with Omar on his first hunting trip. And being with Akhil was one of the few really bright spots in my life these days. My feelings seemed to be reciprocated too. He was treating me more and more like I imagine someone treats a "girlfriend"—holding hands when we walked down the hall, giving me affectionate looks and smiles. He was very natural with it all. I suppose I was the only one who still got butterflies in my stomach half the time.

We'd still been doing everything with Omar. I

wondered if on the camping trip we might actually get some time alone together. But thinking about being alone with him made the stomach butterflies go absolutely berserk, so I thought about what books I wanted to bring with me instead.

We left on Friday afternoon to drive deep into the West Virginia mountains. Sam kept the five-hour drive interesting. He seemed to think that each one of us was on the trip for the sole purpose of watching him get his first buck. He never stopped talking.

"And the day we did target practice—remember?" Sam turned around from the front seat and looked from Omar to Akhil. "Remember the guy who said there's wolves on Middle Mountain?"

The boys both nodded.

Dad shook his head. "I don't think there are wolves in West Virginia," he said. "Plenty of coyotes, eating the sheep and goats and chickens, but—"

Sam interrupted him excitedly. "No! You were talking to Mr. Carson and didn't hear. It was his cousin Jimmy who told us that somebody shot a wolf on Middle Mountain."

"That's what he said," Omar chimed in to explain. "Said the hunter thought it was a coyote, but it turned out to be a white wolf. He got a big fine for killing it too. There's this lady who raised a pack of wolves and released them on Middle Mountain."

Dad whistled. "I didn't know that. I'd like to talk to Jimmy myself, hear the whole story."

"Isn't that . . . where we're camping?" I asked hesitantly.

"Right," said Dad. "Laurel Fork Wilderness is on Middle Mountain."

The boys started howling and laughing. Omar growled and grabbed me with his hands bent like claws.

"Stop it!" I ordered and slapped Omar's hands away. I was going on this trip to escape things that scared me, and I was *not* happy to be finding new things to fear. I hoped Akhil was right about wolves not attacking people.

"Don't worry, Becky," said Sam valiantly. "I'll sleep with my rifle, and if a wolf tries to get you, I'll shoot it between the eyes!" He made a gunshot noise with his mouth.

I didn't even have a moment to smile at Sam's offer of protection before Akhil's hand came down like a clamp on Sam's shoulder and his voice cut through our chatter.

"You will *not* shoot a wolf." Akhil boomed.

"Ow, you're hurting me," Sam wriggled his shoulder free of Akhil's grip.

"There is no reason to harm a wolf," Akhil said more gently. "They are not a threat to us."

"Okay, *fine*," Sam said sulkily.

But a moment later he was back to jabbering about how many points his buck was going to have, and the moment of tension had blown over. We stopped for gas and a bathroom break in Keyser, then began to wind our way into the hills. An almost full moon rose, and the mountains were black silhouettes against a charcoal gray sky.

"Do wolves really howl at the moon?" Sam asked no one in particular.

"No," said Akhil "They howl to announce where they are—to their pack members it means 'come over here!' and to the members of another pack it means 'this is our territory. Stay away!' Sometimes they howl before a hunt, to get themselves psyched up. And sometimes they do it for fun—kind of like a community sing."

I laughed at the community sing idea. "You make them sound like people," I said.

Akhil looked at me thoughtfully. "They're very much like people," he said. He narrowed his eyes. "In some ways they're more human than people."

I scrunched up my face at him.

"Ah—jeez. I don't know what I'm trying to say." He stumbled over his words. "Never mind."

It was almost ten o'clock when we finally pulled into the Laurel Fork campground. Sam had finally quieted down and was looking very sleepy. When he tried to get out of the car, one of his canes slipped and he fell.

"Becky, he's tired," said Dad. "Why don't you help him get ready for bed and me and the older boys will pitch the tents."

I pulled Sam up off the ground. "Want a ride?" I asked. I knew better than to assume that Sam wanted to be carried. Most of the time he insists on doing things for himself. But when he gets really tired his muscles are difficult to control.

"Yeah," he said sleepily.

I carried him to the outhouse and waited outside for him. The air was crisp and cold and smelled of fire. Nearby sat a circle of men dressed in camouflage, their faces lit by a kerosene lamp and a dying campfire. An owl hooted. I shivered. I wondered if we'd hear wolves howling during the night.

I carried Sam back to where our tent was already up. Omar and Akhil were struggling with theirs.

"How's a five A.M. wake-up call sound?" asked Dad.

I groaned.

"Got to be out there at feeding time," Dad said.

"Sounds good to me," said Omar. The other two boys agreed.

I crawled into the tent next to Sam and my dad, determined to sleep through the five A.M. wake-up call, the gunshots, and everything else that happened in the Laurel Fork Wilderness before lunchtime.

sixteen

MAYBE IT WAS the mountain air, or knowing that I was safely far away from Kyle Metzger and his ilk, but it was the longest night's sleep I'd had in a week. I barely remembered Dad and Sam unzipping the tent before dawn. Gunshots made me stir a few times later in the morning, but when I finally stuck my head out to see the day, the sun was high and shining brightly between bare winter branches.

I made a visit to the outhouse, then rummaged around in the cooler in the car for a bagel. I carefully sealed the cooler and covered it with a blanket. Dad had said there are plenty of black bears in the West Virginia mountains, and if they smell food or even see it through a car window, they'll break the windows to get at it.

I heard a creek running nearby, so I grabbed my towel and went to wash. I cupped my hands in the stream, and when I splashed it on my face it was so cold it stopped my breath.

There was no one in the campground. The fire circle of the other hunters lay quietly smoldering. I knew that Dad and the boys had taken crackers and cans of tuna with them and wouldn't be back until suppertime. The bright sunshine made it warm enough to sit at the picnic table to read. I felt free and safe and peaceful. I dug out *The Collected Poems of Edna St. Vincent Millay* and *The Great Gatsby*, which I was reading for the third time, and bundled in ski coat, wool hat, mittens, and a Day-Glo orange vest for good measure, I settled in for the afternoon.

I didn't even hear him approach. By the time Akhil said, "Hi, Becky," he was quite close, and it made me jump. He plopped down next to me on the picnic bench, wrapped both arms around me, and pulled me to him in a hug. It felt warm and cozy, even though I could hardly feel his arms through our heavy jackets. He looked at *The Great Gatsby* open on the picnic table.

"He dies in the end," he said somberly.

I giggled. "He does not. This is the newer version where George has a heart attack and dies before he can shoot Gatsby."

Akhil laughed and leaned back to look at me. He was smiling in a dreamy sort of way. He slipped his warm hand behind my neck and started to pull me toward him. *Oh my God*, I thought, *he's going to kiss me, and I don't know how!*

I panicked. I stiffened, grinned real big, and said, "Did you murder anything?"

Akhil looked startled for a moment, then composed himself and removed his hand from my neck. "I don't think that technically it's murder unless it's within the same species," he said.

The near-kiss had raised my temperature about ten degrees. I pulled off my wool hat and unzipped my coat. "Did you guys get anything for dinner, though?" I asked.

Dad had refused to keep any meat in our cooler because he said the bears would smell that right through the plastic wrapping, cooler, and car doors. We'd eat vegetarian unless they killed something.

"I think it's pasta primavera all the way," said Akhil.

"Not even a rabbit?" I asked mournfully.

Akhil shook his head. "Your Dad got a groundhog in his sights, but then didn't shoot because he said you think groundhog is too greasy and it grosses you out."

I nodded emphatically. "Pasta primavera sounds *perfect*." Then I asked, "Is Sam disappointed?"

"He can't really move quietly with his canes," said Akhil, "but he won't be carried because he says then he wouldn't be a real hunter. And then he doesn't want to sit still for long, and when he does sit, he likes to talk. So we never even saw a deer close enough to shoot at." He shrugged. "He doesn't know he's the reason, though, so don't tell him."

I shook my head. Of course I wouldn't. I could just picture my dad trying to get Sam to sit and be quiet, and Sam's excitement bubbling up, and my dad giving in and letting him talk and move from one spot to another, even though Dad knew they were scaring all the deer away.

"He's in great spirits, though," said Akhil. "Still very hopeful about tomorrow."

Just then we heard something crashing through the forest, and as the sound became louder, there were Dad, Sam, and Omar tromping up the trail.

The sun sank low, and it turned colder. Dad, Sam, and Akhil fixed dinner on the camp stove while Omar and I gathered wood and built a fire. As dusk turned to dark and we sat in a circle around the flames of our fire, holding steaming bowls of pasta, I felt like I wanted to stop time right there. I wanted to stop it before we all moved forward into the next days and weeks. Before Sam found out he wouldn't get a buck this weekend. Before Akhil discovered I'd never been kissed before, so I didn't know how. Before Kyle and Rudy did something horrible and crazy—or never did anything horrible and crazy, but kept me and Omar and Akhil scared to death worrying that they would. Before . . .

"She's having deep thoughts." It was Akhil's voice, and it brought me back from what seemed like far away.

"Either that or she's gone deaf," said Sam irritably.

"Maybe she's tired from whatever she did today. I mean, we don't know *what* she did today, do we?" said Omar.

"How did I suddenly become the topic of conversation?" I demanded.

"No need to get upset, honey," said my dad. "You were just daydreaming and Sam tried to talk to you, that's all."

I blinked, embarrassed. "Sorry, Sammy."

"So, are you listening now?" he asked.

I nodded.

"Do you want to go on a night hike with us? Daddy says just us kids can go as long as we bring flashlights. Do you want to?" The fire lit up his round face, hopeful with anticipation.

Bears come out at night, I thought. Wolves prowl at night. Coyotes, bobcats, even skunks come out at night. But Sam was looking at me with such eagerness . . .

"Okay," I said.

"All right! Let's go," said Sam.

"*Now?*" I squeaked.

"Dishes first," said Dad.

We each washed our own bowl and fork in water from one of the plastic jugs we'd brought from home. It just about froze my hands to get them wet.

While the boys finished putting away the stove and washing the pots, Dad pulled me aside. "Becky, that trail is a mite rocky," he said softly so that Sam couldn't hear. "Go *slowly* and keep a hand on him. If it's too hard in the dark, turn back, all right?"

I promised I'd take good care of Sam, and he gave me a smile that said he knew I would. What he didn't know was that I was actually relieved that it would be slow going with Sam. I hoped we'd get about thirty feet away from the campsite, decide it was too difficult to hike in the dark, and turn back. So I could have strangled Omar when he said, "Sammy—leave your crutches. You can ride piggyback."

"Yippee!" Sam cried.

Omar crouched down so Sam could climb up.

"If Omar gets tired, I'll be your next porter," said Akhil.

"Good deal," said Sam. He grinned as Omar stood up.

I handed out flashlights and tried to think if there was any possible way to stop this excursion, or at least extricate myself from it. But we were obviously on our way, and Dad had put me in charge of Sam, so there was no getting out of it.

I started toward the flat trail they'd taken during the day.

"Becky, come this way," Omar called to me. He was heading the other direction. "We're going up the mountain to find the white wolves."

"Wonderful," I said under my breath. I followed the boys up a steep, rocky path. The full moon was bright enough so that our bodies made ghostly shadows as we walked.

Akhil lagged behind with me and took my hand.

"Are we really trying to find the white wolves?" I asked him.

He shook his head. "That talk is mostly for Sam's benefit. It's nearly impossible to *find* a wolf. They're quite afraid of people, so they run off. I'd love to hear a howl, though." He stopped and looked around us at the dark woods. "It would do my heart good."

Fortunately, before we'd gone much more than a mile, Omar got tired of carrying Sam, Sam got sleepy, and Akhil reminded us that we still had to hike back so we shouldn't go too much farther.

"If you want to find a wolf, the best thing to do is sit still and be silent," said Akhil.

"That sounds good," said Sam. He yawned.

We hiked a little farther up to a group of boulders, glowing white like bones in the moonlight. We found seats among the rocks. Sam cuddled up next to me and laid his head in my lap.

"You warm enough?" I asked.

He nodded and closed his eyes.

"He'll find more wolves than we will," said Akhil, "in

his dreams." He sounded so sad when he said it, I quickly searched his face.

"I can't tell if wolves make you happy or sad," I said.

He rubbed his forehead. "Both, I suppose."

We sat there for a time, listening to the quiet woods, straining to hear something other than the soft rustle of dry leaves in the wind and the rush of a creek nearby.

"Have you heard them ever?" Omar whispered.

Akhil nodded and looked up at the full moon. "Many, many times." His voice broke as he said it, and I saw that his cheeks were glistening with tears.

"Akhil, what—" I began.

"Is he asleep?" Akhil asked.

I stroked Sam's hair, and he stirred slightly but didn't open his eyes. "Yes," I said.

"Then I will tell you," said Akhil "They asked me not to tell, and I have not, for a long, long time. But because of everything . . . we've found out, I can't keep it a secret from the two of you any longer. Will you promise that what I say will stay within the circle of us three?"

Omar and I both nodded solemnly.

"Then I will tell you," said Akhil, "who I am."

seventeen

"I'M NOT THE first one of my kind who has been brought back to live among humans, but I'm the first who has been able to really talk—to tell about what my life was like with *them*."

"I *knew* it!" Omar nearly shouted. "*Aliens!* That's why you've got ESP and all that."

Akhil looked cross. I knew that whatever he had to say, it wasn't easy for him.

"Omar, can we just be quiet and let Akhil tell it?" I said.

Omar nodded and settled back against the rocks. He clasped his hands behind his head and grinned. "I knew it," he said again.

Akhil continued. "The ones before me—Amala and Kamala, and others—they were probably abandoned as infants, and so later they learned only a few words, at best. But the scientists who have studied me think my mother—my human mother—was with me for some time. She must have run away to the forest with me, maybe running from a cruel husband or father, or maybe the shame of being pregnant and unwed—but she must have survived until I was a couple of years old, so that I developed the language centers in my brain."

"And then she was murdered?" I whispered.

Akhil frowned. "No. Who would murder her in the wilderness?" He shook his head. "I don't know. I've tried to piece it together so many times. She might have been attacked by a leopard when she was out hunting while I slept. Or she might have fallen and been injured, and then, unable to move, been eaten by ants. . . ." I saw that perspiration had broken out over his forehead. "I have one vague memory of someone holding me—human, female, loving. But as hard as I've tried, I can't remember her face."

Omar was no longer grinning. He leaned forward. "I thought your parents were murdered," he said.

Akhil blinked at us. "They were. One day I was playing with the cubs—we were waiting for the adults to return with food. A hunter found us. He grabbed me and tied me to a tree—by then I was about five years old. Then he waited in hiding. When the adults returned he lifted his rifle. My mother looked at me, like why was I tied to a tree? He shot her. Blood spurted out onto her fur. He shot the others as they ran—my father, the other pack members. Then he shot the cubs. They were too young to know they should run. I was screaming." Akhil let out a shuddery breath. He was shaking. "It was my fault. I'm sure they picked up the human scent, but they thought it was only me. They walked into the hunter's trap."

I gave Akhil a tissue from my pocket, and he wiped his eyes. "The hunter dragged me back to his house, still tied with that rope. He expected me to become part of his household as a servant. He lived in the village of Narayanpur, near the forest of Musafirkhana where he found me. But I knew him only as the murderer of my family. I made much more trouble than I was worth. He took me to the orphanage in Lucknow, and after a few months there I was speaking Hindi quite well." Akhil blew his nose into the tissue and spoke more calmly. "At some point somebody figured out that I was a rare specimen: the first talking wolf child. I was shipped to the Medical Institute in Delhi to participate in their tests and examinations. Their fascination is mostly about how my brain and senses work. For the first year, my skin was hardly affected by cold or heat. My hearing and sense of smell are very highly developed, and I can still see in the dark.

"After several months, someone in the UK must have pulled some strings, because I was sent to London to the research hospital there. First I learned English, then there were more tests, more examinations. And then this year, the Americans wanted their chance to stick me with needles and ask me thousands of questions, so here I am." He held out his hands, palms up. "The best kept multinational government secret since all those alien carcasses they've got stored in freezers." He wiggled his eyebrows at Omar.

"*Wolf* child?" Omar breathed. "The pack, the cubs, your *parents*—they were all wolves?"

Akhil nodded. "They adopted me, let me keep warm with their cubs in the den, and brought me meat from the kills the same way they brought it to their own cubs."

"So, you had, like, this wolf mother who would come trotting up with a hunk of raw meat in her mouth and drop it in front of you, like you were one of her cubs? *Awesome!*" Omar exclaimed.

Akhil cleared his throat, looking embarrassed. "Well, actually, they don't carry it back in their mouths. They eat it and bring it back in their stomachs."

"So how do you get it?" Omar asked.

"They, uh . . ." Akhil hesitated. "They regurgitate it."

Omar and I both burst out with gasps of disgust. We were so loud, Sam stirred in his sleep.

"Hey, I would have died without them," Akhil said defensively. "And how is a two- or three-year-old human child supposed to chew up raw meat? When they brought it back, it was prechewed, and nice and warm."

That last image almost made me puke on the spot,

but I kept my composure out of respect for Akhil and all he'd been through.

Omar narrowed his eyes at Akhil. "So, was that how you knew what was in my lunch bag—you *smelled* it? It wasn't ESP?"

Akhil nodded. "I always know what's in your lunch bag."

"And that copperhead—you *saw* it in the dark?" Omar asked.

"The one you almost stepped on several weeks ago? Yes, I saw it. But I smelled it too. Copperheads smell like cucumbers."

"Wow," I said. "I am *always* taking you with me when I go hiking in the dark."

"And your scars—are you finally going to tell us how you got them?" Omar asked.

Akhil laughed. "They're from playing with the cubs all day. They play *hard*!"

"What about the sitting-on-the-floor thing, and always sitting cross-legged?" Omar asked.

"My spine formed differently, because I squatted and moved on all fours like I saw my wolf family doing. I've never taken much to chairs—they just don't fit my body."

"Makes sense," said Omar. Then he seemed to suddenly remember Akhil's reference to the alien carcasses stored in top secret government freezers. "The *aliens*, man . . . do they let you see them? Have you touched them? Do they have, like, these big heads and huge eyes, and little tiny mouths—"

"Omar!" Akhil stopped him, laughing. "I was *kidding.*"

"Oh," Omar said, looking deflated.

"So, is my secret safe with you?" Akhil asked.

"Absolutely," I said

"Scouts' honor," said Omar.

We were all quiet for a time, watching the shadows of branches in the moonlight. Then Akhil sighed. "When I die I want my ashes scattered on a mountain where wolves live," he said. "They're the only family I've ever really known. They're the only ones who will mourn for me."

I shuddered. "Good grief, Akhil, by the time you die you'll have kids and grandkids and everything. Don't you want to be buried so they can visit your grave?"

"Hindus don't bury people—at least not common people," he said. "Not that I'm a good Hindu, eating beef and all, but I was introduced to Hinduism at the orphanage, and I like the cremation idea. No rotting flesh or worms crawling in your eye sockets."

"Hey, Akhil," Omar said, interrupting our morbid conversation. "What did you mean that because of all we've found out you couldn't keep this wolf stuff a secret from us anymore?"

Akhil rubbed his hands together to warm them. "Because I needed you to understand that my senses are not ordinary. You need to know that for several years I lived with animals who can smell prey from two kilometers away, who can hear a howl from fifteen kilometers away, and who can sense the invisible boundary lines that divide one pack's territory from another. I learned language from my human mother, but I learned to *sense* from my wolf family. I needed you to understand this and trust me when I tell you what my senses are telling me now."

I looked at him in the silver light. "What are they telling you now?" I whispered.

Akhil looked up at the moon, then at Omar, then at me. "That we three have stumbled upon the plans for a massacre."

eighteen

SAM WOKE ENOUGH to groan that he was cold. Akhil gathered him in his arms, and the three of us hiked down the trail toward camp. In my mind's eye, images crowded in, flashing one after another the way they had flashed on the television newscasts after crazed students at other schools used guns and bombs to take out their anger on their classmates. Except that in the images in my mind now, I recognized the faces. Students huddled together in terror, some of them bleeding—instead of kids from some other state, I saw Dora Melissano and David Kazinsky. A girl lying in a pool of blood—instead of a face and name I didn't recognize, I saw Katrina Bobcheck. Mothers clinging to one another, praying and crying—I saw my mother and Omar's . . .

"What would the wolves do?" I blurted it out into the quiet forest.

The boys stopped hiking and turned to me.

"What?" asked Omar.

I clenched my fists. "The wolves gave you all this

knowledge, this sensing." I sobbed once and quickly wiped my sleeve across my face. "I want them to give us the answers. What are we supposed to *do?* What would *they* do?"

My loud voice had woken Sam up. "Becky, why are you crying?" he asked, rubbing his eyes.

I tried to calm myself down, but fury and frustration rose inside me. "I hate it!" I cried. "These people shoot everyone they want to and then"—I pointed my index finger at my head like a gun—"they shoot themselves. But it doesn't stop until then. And afterward the stupid humans—the schools, the teachers, the parents, other students—say, 'Oh, yeah, I guess he did play violent video games twenty-four-seven and was building pipe bombs in the garage. I guess we should have noticed.' But how can we *stop* them? We can't let it happen!"

Sam reached for me so he could hug me, and I cried into the nape of his neck.

"I want to know," I said more softly, "what the wolves would do."

Akhil wrapped his arms around both me and Sam, and I felt his warm breath in my hair. "We can't do what the wolves would do," he said.

"Why *not?*" I jerked out of his embrace, scowling.

Akhil was surprised by my anger, and it sparked anger of his own. "Because ripping out teenagers' throats is generally frowned upon in human society," he said harshly.

I hugged Sam tighter. "That's what they would do?" I asked weakly.

Akhil nodded.

"The wolves are going to rip out somebody's throat?" Sam asked, trying to make sense of the conversation.

"No," I said. "There are no wolves." I shifted his weight in my arms, but I couldn't hold him much longer.

"Here." Omar took Sam from me and spoke calmly. "I think we should stop telling these scary stories—see, Becky got so scared by that dumb story that she started blubbering and everything." He widened his eyes at me and rolled them toward Sam. "I'll save one more ghost story to tell tomorrow in the car on the way home, but no more tonight, okay?"

Sam nodded sleepily and settled into Omar's arms. I kept my mouth shut, but I was glad that Sam couldn't hear me crying softly as we finished the hike back to camp.

There was no way I could sleep. As I lay in the tent next to Sam and my dad, I went over and over our options, and kept running into brick walls.

Option 1: Call the police.

And tell them what? That Akhil has wolf senses and he knows the future?

Option 2: Tell our parents.

But what could they do about it that we couldn't do?

And my parents had enough burdens, with Sam and debts, and I knew Omar would fiercely protect his mother from what he'd learned about Kyle's beliefs.

Option 3: Alert Dr. Mack and other school officials.

To what? To the fact that Kyle Metzger has a violent temper and violent fantasies? They already knew that, and they knew they'd be sued if they tried to discipline Mr. Metzger's darling boy, even if he did do something. And he hadn't done anything. Yet.

Option 4: Tell Dr. Mack about the article we'd found in Kyle's backpack.

I could just hear Mr. Metzger: "Yes, these children stole my son's backpack, planted this article in it, and now are trying to implicate him. . . ."

Option 5: Give Kyle's notebook to Dr. Mack as evidence.

"And where did you find this, Becky? How do you know it belongs to Kyle Metzger?" "Well, Dr. Mack, it has to belong to him because I found it under the sweaters in his room when I broke into his house. . . ."

Brick walls.

Finally, I got up, wrapped my sleeping bag around my shoulders, and went to see what Omar and Akhil were up to.

"Hey," I whispered loudly outside their tent. "Are you guys asleep?"

I heard Omar groan and saw the light of his pen

flashlight come on. "No, of course not," he said groggily. "It's only . . . two-fifteen A.M. Why would we be sleeping?"

"How can you sleep at a time like this?" I whispered frantically.

"What's going on?" I heard Akhil's confused, sleepy voice.

Omar unzipped the tent. "Well, we're not sleeping now. You might as well come on in."

I crawled inside and plopped myself down between them, bundled in my sleeping bag. "Anybody come up with an idea of what we can do?" I asked.

"I was dreaming that I'd gotten this awesome fire-shooter-laser thing and I was on my way over to Kyle's house to vaporize him," said Omar. He yawned. "Then you woke me up and I never got to do it."

"Sorry," I said. I really was.

Akhil rubbed his eyes, then propped himself up on one elbow and blinked at me. "You look very pretty with your glasses off," he said.

"Oh, God, if you two are going to start flirting, I'm out of here." Omar pulled his sleeping bag over his face.

I could have slugged Akhil. Number one, for giving me a compliment when I was scared out of my mind rather than some time when I could appreciate it; number two, for apparently not thinking I looked pretty with my glasses *on*; and number three, for not immediately offering a brilliant solution to the Kyle Metzger problem. In fact, I could have slugged him *three* times.

"I'm not flirting!" I brought my fists down on my crossed legs. "I want *answers*, not compliments. I *need* answers." My voice cracked and I was afraid I might start crying again.

"I apologize," Akhil said. "You're right. I just couldn't help noticing. Anyway, I did come up with an idea or two before I fell asleep."

"Good," I said.

"I was thinking, Becky, that you're right. We should do what the wolves would do." He held up one hand to stop us from objecting. "But we shouldn't treat them like outsiders, members of another pack. We should treat them like members of our own pack. After all, they still are, aren't they? They go to our school and haven't done anything terrible"—he looked at me—"on purpose."

"What do wolves do with their own pack members who get screwy?" Omar asked.

Ahkil's eyes flashed conspiratorially. He hesitated, making us wait. Then, with a mischievous grin, he said, "They socialize them."

nineteen

IT TURNS OUT that a wolf pack is a community. Wolves have a whole complicated system of keeping pack members in line, letting everyone know who is boss, and making sure everybody cooperates and gets along. Akhil said he remembered some of it. Since he didn't mature the way the wolf pups did, each year he had a new litter of pups to wrestle with and figure out the pecking order of, making sure he didn't end up being the omega wolf—the lowest ranking, who gets nipped at by everybody. But a lot of what he told us he said he'd learned from reading books by people who study wolves. He showed us books with photos of wolves interacting; young wolves licking the muzzles of the adults when they come back from the hunt to get them to give up the fresh meat stored in their stomachs, a courting male and female grooming each other, a lower ranking wolf rolling onto his back to show his belly to the alpha male.

Akhil said that it's the alpha wolves, the highest ranking male and female, who work the hardest to keep the whole pack safe. And it's the juvenile, immature, less responsible (I said that sounds like Kyle all the way) wolves who are lower ranking and get their noses bit a lot to keep them in line.

"Pack members might scuffle a bit, but they don't kill each other," said Akhil. "If we can socialize Kyle and Rudy, show them their place within the pack, show them that we recognize them as *part of* the pack, then I don't see how they could direct violence at their own pack members."

At lunch on Tuesday Akhil was still filling us in on wolf communication. "There is one case where socialization doesn't work—one case in which a wolf doesn't act like a wolf . . . and a human doesn't act like a human," Akhil said. "Insanity."

"Wolves go insane?" I asked, surprised.

"Rabies," said Akhil. "A rabid wolf does crazy things. In fact that's where most of the scary stories about wolves come from, because rabid wolves *have* been known to attack humans—"

"So they *are* dangerous animals," Omar interrupted him.

Akhil gave him an icy glare. "Rabid wolf, rabid Rottweiler, rabid chipmunk—they're all dangerous," he said sternly.

Omar held his hands up in defense. "I get your point," he said.

I blinked at them. I had just seen the whole interaction in wolf language: Omar had done/said something amiss. Akhil took on the dominant role, stared him down, and set him straight *(Growl! Nose bite!)*. Omar, not wanting to fight—we were friends, in the same pack—gave in easily and basically rolled over to show his belly, just like in the photo Akhil had showed us.

"Hey, alpha wolf," I said, smiling, looking straight at Akhil. "I think I'm starting to understand this wolf stuff. And that makes you responsible for the safety of the pack. What do we do now?"

Akhil looked amused by me calling him alpha wolf. He sat up straight with an air of authority. "Now," he said, "you have to do what I say."

I bowed my head and hands at him, worship style, teasing.

"Becky," he said firmly, "*you* have to learn to pull rank on Kyle. Do you realize you subordinate yourself to him every time you pass him in the hall?"

"I *what?*" I was suddenly no longer being entertained by the alpha wolf idea. My outburst got the attention of everyone at the nearby tables.

"Shhh." Akhil leaned in close to me. "Remember what I said about eye contact? Well, Kyle stares you down, and you look away. When you do it, I can almost see you flatten your little pointy ears and tuck your tail between your legs."

I glared at him.

"Perfect. That's *it*. Direct eye contact, don't look away, keep it steady. Do *that*"—he pointed at my scowling face—"next time you pass Kyle in the hall, and you'll be top dog."

I rolled my eyes.

"And don't forget, head high, stand tall, ears up, look alert," he coached.

"Oh, all right," I grumbled. "I can do everything except the ears."

The worst part about Akhil's socialization plan was that I was going to have to stop ignoring Kyle Metzger and actually have contact with him. Akhil promised that all of our contact would be friendly and jovial, the way wolves are most of the time—but that we would be sending a clear, subconscious message to Kyle and Rudy that *we* were dominant and they were subordinate, that we were in control and they were not. He said wolves do it with a lot of nipping, playful growling, nose biting, and rolling around, and that we would find other ways to do it, but that if it would help me get in the mood I could imagine furry, playful wolves wrestling. I told him thank you very much for the vivid mental image.

"All right, so our first plan is"—Akhil held out his hands, his face bright, like he was about to make a very exciting announcement—"riding the bus home together!"

Omar and I just stared at him.

"I don't ride the bus. I ride my bike," said Omar.

"Kyle doesn't ride the bus either," I said. "His father bought him a car."

But Akhil's enthusiasm was not dampened. "Yes, but today we're *all* riding the bus!"

Omar and I stared again.

Akhil continued. "Because Omar's bike will remain safely locked up until Mr. Nuamah drives him back for it, and,"—Akhil's face showed bewildered surprise— "this afternoon Kyle's tires will very mysteriously lose all their air!"

I narrowed my eyes at him. "How will you find his car in the parking lot?"

"I saw where he parked this morning."

"Won't Kyle think it's weird that we're all suddenly riding his bus?" asked Omar.

"And practically sitting in his lap, we're so interested in everything about him? Probably. But that's not the point," said Akhil. He slumped forward, elbows on the lunch table. "Come on, guys, you've got to get with the program. This socialization stuff can be fun—just think of furry—"

"I know, I know," I interrupted him. "Furry, cute, playful wolves rolling around and biting each other on the nose in a most friendly way. What if Kyle doesn't like it?"

"I'm not expecting him to like it," Akhil said. "He just has to endure it."

Omar and I reluctantly agreed to the plan.

"Do you need somebody to do lookout for you while you liberate his tires?" Omar asked.

Akhil shook his head. "No—you two get to class. The teachers actually *care* whether you're late or not."

"They don't care if you're late?" I asked, surprised.

"They only care that I don't disrupt anything. I can come in a half hour late as long as I do it quietly," he said. "They don't think of me as a real student—just some aberration they have to put up with until NIH is done with me." He looked thoughtful. "Which, come to think of it, is the truth."

"But . . ." I began, then didn't know what to say. I hadn't imagined Akhil *leaving*. I thought he'd moved here, would be here for years just like the rest of us.

The end-of-lunch bell left me without time for asking questions, and the three of us agreed to meet in the parking lot near Kyle's forest green Acura right after school.

• • •

A stream of expletives came from the far end of the parking lot as Omar and I hurried to our appointed meeting place. Then came Akhil's calm voice.

"Yeah. That happened to my uncle's car once. This Japanese? Yep. Something about high concentrations of fluorocarbons in the factories over there lowers the conductivity of the air pressure in the tires."

"Bull shit!" Kyle shouted, and went off on another tirade in which the *F* word figured prominently. Rudy was there, hands in his pockets, looking like a cocker spaniel who was getting yelled at for messing on the carpet.

"Hey, no problem," Akhil was saying. He actually tried to put an arm around Kyle's shoulder, but Kyle jerked away and shoved Akhil.

"Off me, fag," Kyle growled.

Akhil looked only a little shaken. "I was just going to say that the buses are still here—how about I go hold yours—you live near Omar, so that's bus number fifty-two, right? I'll go ask the driver to wait."

By now Omar and I were close by, but neither of us wanted to fully enter the scene. We leaned against a white utility van two rows away.

"Friendly wolf pups, right?" I said under my breath.

"Werewolves," Omar said. Then he stood up straight and squared his shoulders. "Well, here goes," he said, and walked into the fray.

"Hey Kyle, hey Rudy, how's it going?" Omar sang out. "Nice car—something the matter?"

"Nothing I want to talk to you degenerates about," Kyle responded. "Just *clear out*"—he looked over at me—"and take your ugly girlfriend with you."

Kyle ducked into his car, and I saw him dialing a cell phone. Amazingly, Omar and Akhil stayed put. They talked quietly to Rudy, who looked like he was being reasonable. As Kyle got out of his car, Akhil waved and backed away. "Good idea—call triple A or whatever. Guess you don't need the bus after all, so I won't say anything to the bus driver. See you guys in school tomorrow—maybe we can have lunch together or something. Bye Kyle, bye Rudy."

Kyle flipped him the bird.

"Good Lord," I breathed as the two of them joined me to slump against the utility van.

"Well, that went like clockwork, eh?" Akhil said cheerfully.

I gave him a sideways glance. "I hope you're being sarcastic."

"Unfortunately, I am," Akhil said, looking deflated.

"At least Rudy wasn't a jerk," said Omar.

"Yes," said Akhil. "We'll try again with Kyle. But with Rudy, there's definitely hope."

I didn't ask if that meant there was no hope for Kyle. I didn't want to know.

twenty

ALL I *REALLY* had to do, Akhil said, was stop acting subordinate to Kyle. If I didn't want to talk to him that was fine—he and Omar would take care of the serious wrestling and nose biting. For me, looking Kyle straight in the eye, after all he'd done to my family, would be hard enough. Akhil reminded me that it shouldn't be a stare down—staring, among wolves and people, could be taken as a threat or a challenge and could start a fight. Just simple, friendly, steady eye contact. That would assert my confidence and, as someone who cared more about the common good of everybody than Kyle did, establish me as higher ranking than Kyle. I knew I had to give it a try.

It was always the same place, at the same time of day that Kyle passed me, with me coming upstairs from English in a sea of other students, and him on his way downstairs. Sometimes we crossed in the hallway, but sometimes we passed on the steps, which made it awfully easy for him to look down on me and for me to keep my eyes on my feet.

Just look at him, I kept saying to myself. *Assert your authority, your rank as a caring member of society.* Then, all that ranking and responsibility philosophy got too tiresome, and I decided to just think of wolves.

As I walked down the hallway, I felt my muscles and bones move smoothly and tried to feel graceful, like a she-wolf in a forest. I spotted Kyle above me on the steps. I gazed up. *Shoulders back, head high, direct eye contact.* I heard Akhil's words in my mind, saw the she-wolf in a confident stance.

I looked right at him, my face relaxed and friendly. He stared—his usual intimidation stare. As we drew closer, I kept my gaze on him and willed myself to stay calm inside. Do wolves smile, I wondered? I felt so strong, I was about to say "Kyle, how's your car doing?" But he dropped his eyes, looked to the side, and scooted past me, trying to speed by the slower students.

My mouth dropped open and I stopped walking until someone jostled me because I was blocking traffic. Like magic, the tables had turned. Kyle had looked away from *me*.

I couldn't wait to tell Omar and Akhil, but I wouldn't see them until lunch. I was actually curious to see if I looked different, so I slipped into the girls' room for a glance in the mirror. Nope. Same old Becky.

Alana came out of a stall, and I felt myself go into my usual "make yourself small, get out of here before she insults you too badly" routine. I looked down, pretending to search for something in my purse. Then, suddenly, I realized what I was doing—what I'd been doing around Alana and Kathy for years. I squared my shoulders, took a deep breath, then looked up—looked right into Alana's eyes.

"Hello, Alana, how are you?" I said. I smiled. *Nose bite, friendly growl.*

"Okay," she said in a supremely distracted way. She turned her attention to her reflection in the mirror.

"Too bad we don't have any classes together this year, huh?" I said. *Wrestle, nip, nip.* I caught her eyes in the mirror.

"Whatever," she said, annoyed. Then she looked down, busily searching for something in her purse. Pretending to search?

"Well, I've got to go. See you around," I said.

I fairly floated out of the girls' room and into the hallway. They didn't have to like it, they didn't have to respond in a friendly way, they only had to endure it, Akhil had said. And both Kyle and Alana had looked away first. For a few golden moments, I had been top dog!

When lunchtime finally arrived, I rushed to our table, where Omar and Akhil were already sitting.

"This is so cool, I've got to tell you guys—" I began excitedly. But the long looks on their faces stopped me

short. "Something's wrong," I said. My stomach tightened.

"Akhil thinks we might not have time to socialize
Kyle," said Omar. "Like it would take fifty years."

Akhil slouched in his seat. His lip was swollen, and a
cut in it still oozed blood.

"What happened?" I asked.

"We made another attempt at being friendly," said
Omar. "We asked Kyle about his car and tried to have a
nice conversation about did he have a good weekend
when he went away with Rudy because his mom said he
was all excited about it."

"And we got this," said Akhil pointing to his mouth.

"Ouch," I said.

"The one piece of good news is that Rudy walked up
while it was happening and instead of storming off with
Kyle, he stayed and talked with us," said Omar.

"He said to tell you you're not ugly," said Akhil.

"What?!" I exclaimed, wide-eyed.

"Yesterday, Kyle said you were ugly. Rudy apologized
for him."

"Jeez." I waved it away. "If insults were the worst Kyle
Metzger had ever done to me and my family I'd be
happy. I'd be *ecstatic*," I said.

"Anyway, Rudy said that Kyle has been really jumpy
lately, and he thanked us for offering to help yesterday,"
said Omar.

"Good thing they didn't find out we *caused* the problem," I said quietly.

"Yeah, but overall, we're trying to prevent a bigger problem," said Omar.

I looked at Akhil. His lip was even fatter than it had been a couple of minutes ago. "Ice?" I asked.

"Please," he said.

I filled a napkin with ice from the soda machine and brought it back to the table.

"If we don't have time to socialize him, what do we do?" I asked.

"Pee all around the perimeter of the school so he knows it's our territory and he stays out," said Omar.

I gave him an exasperated look.

"Just trying to lighten things up," Omar said in self-defense.

Akhil had brightened. "I think you might be on to something there," he said. "A wolf message in pee gets sent one day, and can be sniffed—or received—days later. Does that *remind* you of anything?"

I hung my head in my hands. "We have a serious situation here, and all you can do is talk like you're in a locker room. This is *not* helping."

"E-mail," said Omar. "Computer-use records. I'm on to you."

"Could you guys please speak in plain English?" I asked.

"There's this one computer in the library those two always mess around on during their lunch and sometimes after school," said Omar. "If we can get onto that computer we can track where they've been—chat room sites, Web sites, stuff like that."

"Yes," said Akhil. "We'll sniff out where they've been."

I still didn't see how they got from pee to computers, but I was glad they had come up with another idea for doing something about the problem. As we left the lunchroom, Omar chattered about animals and pee messages. "I guess if your dog watches you flush the toilet, he thinks you're making a long-distance call, huh?"

twenty-one

OMAR SAID HE'D done more Internet surfing and found out that in a number of schools around the country, kids had told school officials when they thought someone was planning violence, and the school had been able to keep the violence from happening. Most of the time, the kids who blew the whistle had been in on the planning, so they weren't guessing like we were. But he thought we should at least try to lead Dr. Mack to some of the clues we had picked up—or better yet, pick up some new clues that didn't have anything to do with our breaking-and-entering fiasco, and get the information to Dr. Mack.

Omar went into the main office under the guise of picking up PSAT information, did a little snooping around, and found Dr. Mack's E-mail address on a memo to a secretary. Then he insisted that we create an E-mail address using a fake name and send information to Dr. Mack through that. The article he'd read from Kyle's backpack had left him with vivid images of the baseball bat murder of an innocent black man, done in the name of "taking back America," and he refused to let any of our real names be used.

We met in the library after school, and while we waited for Kyle and Rudy to finish on the computer, Omar asked Akhil to tell us about his life with the wolves.

"You mean how Kipling-esque was it?" Akhil asked, smiling slightly. "Not very. I remember we lived in the most cozy, dark cave. I suppose that's how my eyes developed for seeing in the dark. We slept during the day and went out at night. The cubs and I slept in a puppy ball, all curled up together. I still remember the feel of their soft fur and the smell of puppy breath." He looked sad. "I missed them so much, after they'd all been killed. Sleeping in a *bed* was so foreign, so lonely.

"I remember their voices—our voices, really, because I did my best to howl along with them—rising into the chill night air. It was such a feeling of . . . wholeness, like I was part of the magic, like I was *home*." He twisted his hands together. "I still have fantasies of leaping at that damn hunter and sinking my teeth into his neck, ripping out his throat wolf-style before he could shoot my family. I bit him good and hard a few times when he was trying to make me into a servant. Took a nice chunk out of his leg one day. I still remember the taste of his blood and the feeling of victory. He sent me to the orphanage in self-defense."

"Nice going," said Omar. "So you acted just like a wolf. Did you go around on your hands and knees to imitate them too?"

"Hands and knees for short distances, like down a hill to lap up water from a stream. And yes, I lapped it up like they did, never cupped it with my hands. But I traveled bent over on hands and feet for running fast. Man, those people at the orphanage could never catch me when I wanted to bolt. It was a good thing they had walls around the place, or I would have been *gone*, back to the forest. Probably would have starved to death without my wolf family to take care of me."

I was thankful when Kyle and Rudy left the library and we could move to their computer. Akhil's stories about his wolf life made me so sad. It was like there was this sparkling lost world he could never go back to.

Omar sat down in front of the computer. "Okay," he said. "I've created a fake E-mail identity so we can safely send information to Dr. Mack without Kyle or his father coming after us."

Omar opened "history" and we scrolled down the list of Web sites. Most of them had only innocuous-sounding words in the titles. In fact, a lot of them sounded like churches. Then, when we logged on to the sites, we were met with the foulest hate propaganda I had ever seen. We were silent as Omar scrolled and moved from site to site.

"All right, but this is old news," I said. "We already know he believes this stuff."

"Right," said Omar. "But now we have a chance to let Dr. Mack know, let him see for himself, without letting Kyle and his father deny everything."

He opened up an E-mail box and started typing. "We'll tell him to watch which computer Kyle and Rudy use, then check out the history for himself. Then there can't be any 'that hate article doesn't belong to my son' or 'I've never seen that notebook before in my life.' Just let Dr. Mack see it himself." He finished the E-mail and sent it.

We continued down the list, opening a site here and there. One contained an article, "Construction of Pipe Bombs and Other Simple Explosives."

"Make sure to tell Dr. Mack about that one," said Akhil.

Omar opened the article, and the three of us began to read. Halfway down the page, I gasped. "*Glass!*" I said. "They use broken glass as shrapnel. My God, that's why he had it in his closet."

Omar immediately opened an E-mail box. "If we were in on the planning, we'd know about the glass, wouldn't we? Just like those kids who were whistle-blowers. Maybe Dr. Mack should pay a little unannounced visit to the

Metzger household and take a peek in Kyle's closet. I'll suggest it."

When Omar had sent the E-mail, I felt good, hopeful, like we were finally doing the right thing. That was on the afternoon of December eleventh.

twenty-two

WHO CAN TELL why sometimes people just *know* things? Like the girl I read about who was killed in a school shooting a few years back. A year before she died, she wrote in her diary, "This is my last year, Lord." And that very morning she said something to her mother like, "What will you do without me?"

I don't think there is a logical explanation as to why I woke up that day and the Latin numbers duo duodecidem, which had meant two-twelve, February twelfth, in my head for so long, suddenly rearranged themselves into two *twelves*, twelve twelve: December twelfth. I awoke in a cold sweat, sat up in bed, and I *knew*.

Omar's phone was busy, but I left a message on Akhil's cell phone to meet me in front of our English classroom as soon as he got to school. Then I ran to the bus stop to make sure I didn't miss the bus.

Akhil had said that if we still hadn't gotten anywhere with Kyle or with Dr. Mack by February 12, we'd just set off the fire alarms right when we got to school, so we'd get everybody outside in case of a bomb. We had to do that *today*.

When I got to school Akhil was waiting for me.

"This is it," he said.

I could tell from the look in his eyes that his wolf sense had told him the same thing that I now knew.

"The alarms," I said "We need to set them off!"

He nodded. He took my hand and led me, running, down the hall. At that moment, a part of me said, loudly, *Becky, you're such an idiot.* Here I was, running down the hall to find some fire alarms, holding hands with Akhil like secret agents in a James Bond movie, when everything in the entire school was perfectly normal. My mind was just gearing up for a lengthy *Becky, this is the stupidest thing you've ever done* lecture, when it hit.

A blast like thunder seemed to detonate inside my head, and the floor tiles sent shock waves up through my feet. Fire alarms wailed as Akhil and I hit the floor.

"Oh God, it's starting," I screamed over the mayhem.

"Main office!" Akhil shouted.

Main office. Dr. Mack. With the list of grievances Kyle held against Dr. Mack, I knew Akhil expected to find him there.

We scrambled to our feet. Frantic students and teachers poured into the halls. Smoke billowed up the stairwell. We held our breath and ran down the smoke-filled staircase. Downstairs water covered the floor and fire sprinklers drenched us with their spray. The din of the alarms made it hard to think.

Outside the main office two panic-stricken secretaries blocked the doors. "Stay out!" one told us. "He has a gun . . . he said everybody out . . . except—"

"Dr. Mack," I finished her sentence for her. I elbowed past her and shoved open the door.

Kyle stood over him, grinning, holding a black handgun. "Now I get even. Now I get to express *my* opinion and *you* have to listen."

Dr. Mack lay on the floor, his face a ghastly white. He gazed, glassy-eyed, up at Kyle. With his right hand he held his left shoulder, and blood seeped between his fingers, dripping onto the floor.

Kyle was so involved with his horrible torture that he paid no attention to us. "See if you like how this feels," he said in a mocking, sticky tone. He held the gun at arm's length, aimed at Dr. Mack's knee, pulled the trigger. Dr. Mack's body jolted in agony. He curled onto his side, cried out.

Akhil crossed the floor in two steps. "Give me the gun!" he shouted over the screaming of the alarms.

Kyle turned his head. His eyes flickered from Akhil to me and back to Akhil. His lips curled in a snarl and the arm that held the pistol moved smoothly to aim at Akhil. Akhil dove at him. The gun blasted. Akhil landed in a heap on the floor.

There was no thought, just movement. I lunged. The image in my mind was of a she-wolf leaping. I hit Kyle with all of my 165-pound bulk. He toppled. His head smacked first the edge of a desk, then the tile floor with a thwack I could hear even over the alarms. I landed on top of him, and in the moment when his eyelids fluttered, I wove my fingers into his hair and, jerking his head up and down with all the violence in my being, slammed the back of his head into the floor over and over again.

"Becky, stop." A familiar voice broke through my rage. "You're done. He's out cold. We have to get them out of here. It . . . smells funny."

It was Omar. He took the pistol from Kyle's limp hand, stuffed it into his own jeans pocket, and began to drag first Dr. Mack, then Akhil, toward the door.

I quickly stood and helped him. As soon as we opened the door to the hallway several students and teachers took over with Dr. Mack. I lifted Akhil's legs, Omar grasped his shoulders, and together we ran outside. Akhil was conscious, and he grunted as we ran with him, but his lips were ghostly pale and his eyes looked dazed.

Outside, students and teachers were milling around, looking shell-shocked and confused. We heard sirens in the distance. I bent down to talk to Akhil.

"An ambulance will be here any minute," I assured him. He was shivering. I took off my sweater and laid it over his chest. Blood had soaked through his clothes on the side of his abdomen. "Looks like he got you in the gut—not the chest or anything. You'll be fine," I said softly.

He looked up at me. "You felt it," he said. He smiled weakly. "The rage—the feeling that something is so wrong, you have to make it right. It's what you saw in me and it scared you. But you felt it." He took a shuddery breath, and I held him to try to warm him. "Now it won't scare you anymore," he said.

Omar called for more sweaters and jackets, and kids wrapped them around Akhil's legs and body.

"Becky." Akhil said it urgently. I looked into his eyes, but instead of speaking, he slid his hand onto the back of my neck, pulled me down gently, and kissed me—just like that, in front of everybody, soft and sweet. I pulled back, embarrassed, but then I leaned in and kissed him again.

The few kids who were gathered around us applauded. "He can't be feeling too bad!" one guy said. "Yeah— and I bet he's feeling even better now," said another. Omar added, "You're going to be *fine*, man." I blushed a deeper red than I've ever been in my life.

Sirens blared close by and two ambulances careened into the parking lot. I looked around me for the first time and saw small knots of people gathered around other wounded students and teachers, pressing wadded-up shirts against bleeding limbs and heads, comforting them, trying to keep them warm. I looked questioningly at Omar.

"The bomb downstairs," he said. "It was in Mr.

Downie's science classroom. I'll tell you later."

We gladly handed Akhil over to the rescue squad and told him we'd visit him in the hospital as soon as we could. Then, just when Omar and I had a moment to take a deep breath, just when the fire alarms had been shut off and a calm had begun to settle because competent EMTs were bandaging the wounded and loading them into ambulances, just when we thought it was *over*, a blast shattered the air, blew out school windows, sent glass flying, sent everyone screaming and diving for the ground.

I lay facedown in the grass next to Omar, arms over my head. When I was sure the explosion was over, I cautiously felt the side of my head—the side that had been toward the blast—afraid of feeling the stickiness of blood. No cuts. No glass. Just my ears ringing loudly.

"You all right?" I asked Omar.

He nodded and propped himself up on his elbows. We both looked back at the school, where smoke was rising from the shattered windows, and the fire alarms were again screeching their warnings. In the same moment the thought came to each of us and our eyes locked. The blast had come from the main office. We had pulled Dr. Mack and Akhil out of there but had left Kyle on his own. We had no way of knowing if he had regained consciousness and gotten himself out before the bomb went off.

twenty-three

THERE WERE TWO funerals in one week. Kyle's was first. They had to use his dental records to identify his body.

My mom and dad said there would have been many more funerals if Omar, Akhil, and I hadn't done what we'd done. Omar said that on his way to math class that morning he'd seen Kyle and Rudy running down the hallway. Rudy had looked right at Omar and shouted "Run!" Omar had smelled something strange—acrid, a little like fireworks. Instead of running, he'd rushed into his classroom, where the smell was coming from, and screamed, "Bomb! Get out!" Then he ran. All of the kids and Mr. Downie were out of the room before the bomb went off. A few people got hit with the flying glass and debris, but that was the worst of it.

Rudy couldn't go to Kyle's funeral. He was in police custody. Omar said he's sure Rudy was supposed to be with Kyle in the office torturing Dr. Mack, and then join him in the rest of what they had planned, whatever that was. But Rudy had defected, first by warning Omar, and then by dropping his gun, which was later found in a hallway, and running until the police found him exhausted and incoherent, in a parking lot in D.C. somewhere. Omar said it was the socialization that broke him, that made him part of our pack so he couldn't go through with their vicious plans.

Omar and I were both questioned by the police as well, especially Omar because he'd been the one to yell, "Bomb!" and because he had a gun in his pocket when the police arrived. But our answers—mine, Omar's, Rudy's, and Akhil's when they talked to him in the hospital—worked together to clear Omar, and he didn't even have to get a lawyer.

When the story ran in the newspaper, there was a statement from Dr. Mack, speaking from his hospital bed, saying that Omar, Akhil, and I had done the right thing in trying to tell him what we'd found out about Kyle and Rudy's plan. He only wished there had been more time to do something about it. And a short article in the B section told about how Mr. Metzger was suing the drug company that makes the antidepressants Kyle was on. He insisted it must have been a side effect of the drug that made Kyle act so crazy.

I only wondered for a minute about whether or not I was responsible for Kyle's death. Sure, I'd knocked him unconscious, but I hadn't set the bomb, and it was the bomb that killed him. I did wonder, though, whether if he'd lived, his father would have been able to get him off the hook for this one. First-degree murder.

The second funeral was three days after Kyle's. At first the people at the hospital said, "the surgery went well," but two days later they said, "peritonitis," and they downgraded his condition from "stable" to "critical." Then they said "systemic infection" and moved him to intensive care. The last thing they said was, "We're so very sorry."

It felt like he slipped through our fingers. We tried to hold on. Omar and I called, asked if we could visit, but always his condition was worse, and they refused to put our calls through, refused to let us see him. And then it was over, and my brain still could not absorb that he was gone.

My thoughts would not rest. If only I had leapt at Kyle *before* he'd aimed at Akhil. If only I'd been able to knock the gun out of his hand. If only we'd figured out weeks ago that we had just until December twelfth to tell Dr. Mack what was going on. If only . . .

In the morning when I was just drifting out of sleep, it felt like he was still there, would be there to grin at me as I walked into English class, or to hang an arm around my shoulders as we left the lunchroom. Then, like mist dissolving in the light of day, the sweetness would disappear and I'd wake up into the nightmare.

My dad said there was work to be done, and it might

help me to focus on that. So he and Omar helped me plan a Hindu funeral service. The priest at the temple said the funeral would be held at a crematorium, and that the closest male relative or friend would light the funeral pyre that would burn Akhil's body. I fell apart when he said that. My dad held me as I sobbed. I said I could not be there while they burned him—I just couldn't. My dad smoothed my hair and said, "You don't have to go, honey. We'll take care of it."

So the rest of my family went to the service and I stayed home. Omar told me there were lots of other people there too: Mr. Nuamah, doctors from NIH, Akhil's host family, and so many students and teachers that you would have thought Akhil was actually well liked at school. Dr. Mack sent a huge bouquet of flowers from the hospital. Omar said that Alana asked about me and said to tell me she was very sorry that I'd lost such a close friend.

They brought Akhil's ashes back in a cold metal urn that weighed heavily in my hands and matched the heaviness around my heart. Omar sat with me as I held the urn. "The priest said fire is a purifier," he said. He put both arms around me and rocked me slightly. "It set his spirit free. And we chanted prayers in Hindi—to help him along his path to his next stage of life."

Tears streamed down my cheeks. "*Life?*" I asked. All I had felt for days was death.

Omar nodded. "We're supposed to keep a lamp lit for thirteen days now, to light his way."

"Like he's still *here*?" I asked, shuddering.

Omar held me tighter. "Like he's on his way to be reborn in another life."

I took a ragged breath. "We have to scatter these," I said.

"I know," said Omar.

• • •

We were quiet on the long drive. At first my dad tried to talk, saying happy things about how much fun we'd all had on that last hunting trip, and how that's the way we should remember Akhil. But neither Omar nor Sam nor I felt much like talking, so my dad soon fell silent as well.

By the time we reached the Laurel Fork Wilderness, it was nearly dark, and a light snow had begun to fall. "There's a road to the top of Middle Mountain," said my dad. "We'll drive up. No use trying to hike up in this weather."

At the top of the ridge, Dad pulled the car over and stopped. The mountains fell away, layer upon layer, their dark hulks patterned against the lightly falling snow and pale sky.

"It has to be in water," I said. "We have to find a creek."

We walked in silence, except for the tap-tapping of

Sam's canes, listening for the sound of one of the many creeks and springs. When I heard the rushing water, my heart jumped. I was about to let go of the last bit of Akhil that I could hold on to.

We hiked down to where a spring flowed right out from the rocks, forming a pool and then a waterfall. We chanted the prayers in Hindi as best we could—prayers to send Akhil's spirit on its way to new life. I opened the urn and shook the ashes—out into the snowy air, down into the flowing water, away from the physical world that I still had to live in. And as the last ashes fell from the urn, and our chanting ended, we heard it.

It filled the forest with its clear, eerie sound. First one howl. Then an answer. Then many voices rising together—wolf voices. A family of wolves. Akhil's family. They sounded so hollow, so mournful, that I thought surely they must be mourning the loss of one of their own, as Akhil had said only they would.

But in the wild night air, the wolves' voices intertwined, gathered energy from one another, raised to a higher pitch, and as the last jubilant howl rose and fell, I knew what they were saying. They were welcoming Akhil home.

author's note

THE PACK IS a work of fiction, yet there is much within it that is true: the awful reality of school violence, the easy availability of guns and bomb-making recipes. While there is no easy answer to the problem of school violence, there is one hopeful note that I found in my research: In recent years, there have been several incidents where school violence has been averted because students who suspected or knew that the violence was being planned went to authorities and alerted them.

Also true in this story is the information about the Holocaust, wolf behavior, and Amala and Kamala and other wolf children. There is one part of this novel that is based on a true story. In 1972, a little boy was found by a hunter in the forest of Musafirkhana in India, playing with the wolf cubs who were his family. The child was tied to a tree by the hunter and watched in horror as the adult wolves returned from their hunt and were shot dead. Then the cubs were shot. Finally the boy was dragged on a rope back to the hunter's home. Later he was taken to the orphanage in Lucknow. When I made that boy into Akhil, my fictional character, I began at the orphanage and let Akhil's story unfold from there.

Are wolves dangerous to humans?

Akhil's statement that healthy wolves don't hunt people and they don't eat people is essentially true. In fact, in North America there has never been a documented case of a wild wolf killing a person. However, to be very accurate, over the past four hundred years there have been rare cases in which wolves have killed humans. These incidents occurred in remote areas of Europe and Asia, and the victims were most often small children who had been left unattended. There are also reports of attacks in areas where wolves have interbred with dogs. These wild wolf-dog hybrids are more dangerous than wolves because they combine the instincts of wolves, who hunt to eat, and dogs, who are not afraid of humans.

For more information about wolves, visit the International Wolf Center Web site at **www.wolf.org**.

For more information about the complex issue of school violence, explore the following resources:

- A violence prevention guide from MTV and the American Psychological Association helps teens recognize the warning signs of violence in themselves and others: **http://www.helping.apa.org/ warningsigns/ index.html**

- The National Crime Prevention Council's Web site provides helpful guidelines on school violence prevention for students, parents, teachers, school officials, law enforcement, and communities: **http://www.ncpc.org/ 2schvio.htm**

- The FBI report, *The School Shooter: A Threat Assessment Perspective*: **www.fbi.gov/publications.htm**

- The Department of Education report, *Early Warning, Timely Response: A Guide to Safe Schools:* **http://www.ed.gov/offices/OSERS/OSEP/Products/ earlywrn.html**

- The Center for Effective Collaboration and Practice Web site contains links to many helpful resources: **http://cecp.air.org/school_violence.htm**